Behind Bars

Behind Bars

**Dorsey Butterbaugh
James Willey**

Dedicated to the customers and staff of Smitty McGee's.

The places are real... the people are not.

Acknowledgements:

The authors would like to thank all those who read the manuscript and gave their unbiased comments, hard as they were to sometimes take. A special thanks to Frank Minni, President of the Rehoboth Beach Writers' Guild, who taught us that the largest key on a keyboard should be the delete button.

There's a fine line between reality and fantasy.*

It's called the bar.

* From *Animal Q*.

It writes itself!

FOREWORD

Writers are often asked where they get their ideas for a story. What was the trigger? What was the seed that started the flow of thoughts? How did the idea grow and then mature into a final product? It's an interesting line of questions. For *Behind Bars*, it was rather simple. It was a quiet night at Smitty McGee's–quiet defined by a lower than normal decibel level–one where you could talk to the person next to you without being hoarse at the end of the night.

Which is what we were doing on a cold blustery night in February 2007. D was making notes on small pieces of paper spread before him. J came by to refill the empty glass sitting amongst the papers and asked in a most polite fashion just what the hell D was doing.

D said he was taking notes for a project he was working on.

"A project... what sort of project?"

Taking a sip of his now overfilled glass, D said, "I'm working on an idea for a book."

J, whose attention span was usually short, sat back on his heels. His eyes lit up. "A book... what kind of book?"

D shrugged his shoulders. "Not sure yet, but probably a novel based on being at the beach."

J scanned the bar to make sure there were no empties needing his attention, then refocused back on D. "I'm thinking about writing a book."

"Oh, yeah. What's yours about?" D inquired.

"The bar business."

"The bar business... very interesting," D said. "What's it about?"

"A collection of observations, bar episodes and commentary generated by the people who come into Smitty McGee's," J explained. "Not a tell-all book, but more of a series of snapshots of what goes on, in and around a bar.

"Doesn't there need to be some sort of a story or plot?" D asked.

"We can mix your story in with my stuff."

"So these observations, etc., will be connected by the story and the main characters?"

"If you say so."

D laughed. "Does this book have a title?"

J nodded and answered the question.

Both men smiled and looked down at the papers on the bar. It was obvious each was entertaining similar thoughts. J did an about face, stepped away and returned a moment later with a bottle of B&B and two empty shot glasses.

A toast was made. *Behind Bars* was born.

1

Mid-March 2007
Fenwick Island, Delaware

The sun had risen to a level where light was able to squeeze through the space between the window drapes. The warmth settled on the face of the lone person spread- eagled across the disheveled bed. He wore a peaceful smile. He was in that state of sleep where dreams were frequent, colorful and vivid. In this dream he was not alone. He let out a soft moan. The pleasure he was experiencing was as intense as the warmth on his cheeks. He adjusted his hips and turned away from the window. Another moan escaped as his dream girl continued her task. It had been a long time since someone–so beautiful no less–had been between his legs. It had been a long time since anyone had even shared his bed.

The sensation continued until he heard a noise–a banging kind of noise–a noise that disrupted his dream. There were several voices. Someone was shouting. The banging grew louder. Suddenly, there was a loud crash, followed by a series of screams.

He tried ignoring the interruptions, redirecting his attention back to his dream. It felt so good; he wanted it to last forever. But it would not be. There was a loud rap on the door. "Uncle Bobby... Uncle Bobby," a small voice called out in panic.

He sat up in bed. He was alone, his dream girl gone.

Tanzania, Africa

For the first time since the surgery began seventeen hours earlier, pediatric neurosurgeon Dr. Adam Singer was able to scratch the itch behind his ear. It was the same itch he always got near the end of a marathon case. Today was no different and he worked at the irritation with his little finger. He was just over six foot tall and trim, with well-defined arm muscles. He had been quite handsome in his earlier years, but as he crossed the golden age of thirty, the good looks slowly evolved into a more mature appearance accentuated by the stress from the long hours on the job and fewer hours in the bed.

Disposing of his gloves and surgical gown, he continued to scratch the ear as he exited the operating room. Calls of *thank you, Dr. Singer* followed him through the doors. Accolades from other members of the Johns Hopkins conjoined surgical team continued as he walked down the corridor. He ran his hand through his short-cropped hair to fluff up the areas flattened by the sweat-soaked surgical cap. While valiant, it was a wasted effort. He wiped his hand on the seat of his scrubs as he prepared to meet the family. He had made it clear before the operation that he would meet with the family first. Only then would he talk to the press. It had always been his rule, regardless of the surgical outcome or the public's interest in the case. Today, the news was good. The conjoined twins, connected at their heads since birth, had been successfully separated. It had been a grueling and tedious operation laced with periods of terror as unexpected anatomical roadblocks were encountered. Each roadblock, however, was tackled with a calmness and determination that had come to be expected from his world-renowned team.

Through a final set of doors, Dr. Singer braced himself for the heat that would surely attack his already sweaty body. (Thank God, the operating room suite was air conditioned, even though the rest of the hospital was not.) He wondered just how many people were waiting. Usually, every family member available came to the hospital and held the vigil. He had little doubt today would be any different. One more hand through his hair, he sucked in a deep breath and entered the waiting room. In spite of his overall fatigue, he wore a smile. It was the expression he wanted the family to see. The smile would immediately answer the question that was first and foremost on everyone's mind: "Are the babies okay?"

He took a few steps forward and glanced around. The room was empty. Dr. Singer looked over his shoulder to make sure he had come out the correct set of doors. Facing forward again, he blinked several times to ensure his fatigue was not playing tricks on him.

Then he realized he was not alone. He refocused and saw Carol Johnston, his administrative assistant, leaning against a side wall. She was dressed in a plain white blouse and khaki shorts. The ever-present glasses sat partway down her nose. He was somewhat surprised to see her. She often traveled with him on high profile cases, but always remained in the background. The reason, she would say with her own signature smile, was to avoid stealing any of his publicity with her good looks.

Today, something was different. She was not her usual kept self. Her hair, normally in a ponytail, was disheveled. Sweat marks were visible on her blouse. And... there was no smile. The look on her face was one he could not recall seeing before. His own smile evaporated as she walked towards him. He suddenly realized roles had been reversed. Instead of the surgeon greeting the family, he was the one waiting to hear the news.

"Adam," she said. She never called him Adam. The news was not good.

2

Spring 2008
Fenwick Island, Delaware

Adam sat and stared out the patio door across the empty lots, past the tree line and across the water. At times his vision was focused. Mostly, however, all he saw was a blur. This is how he passed the time—minute by minute, hour by hour, day by day. Just how many days had past, he was unsure. Then again, it didn't matter. He didn't have anything to look forward to. He didn't have anything to do. Basic daily needs were met... sometimes. Otherwise, his time was spent sitting and staring, his mind as vacant as the lots behind his house. It was his way of coping. It was the only way to avoid the pain. He knew that life could be cruel. He had certainly witnessed enough of that throughout his career. However, what he never really appreciated was just how painful the process.

And so he sat, day in and day out...minute by minute...hour by hour.

Then one day he told himself he should get up

and go for a walk. With little hesitation, he grabbed a jacket, slapped a hat on top of his unruly hair and headed out the door. It was the first time he been out of the house except to go to the store in over a year.

He told himself maybe he should just go for a ride, but argued against that. He needed to walk. Something told him that walking would help the pain, the fresh air would clear his mind. Something told him it was time to move on... or at least make a start in that direction. So that overcast day in April, he took the first step.

Fear quickly engulfed him. Fear of *what w*as unclear, but he was afraid nonetheless. The further he ventured from the house, the more anxious he became. His heart pounded. His palms became sweaty. He felt lightheaded. He told himself to keep going, to keep moving, one step at a time... away from the past and into the future.

The first day he simply walked around the house picking up twigs and other debris spread about from a storm the night before. The second day, he ventured off his property, down to the corner and over to the community pool where he stood outside the fence looking at the vacant body of water surrounded by bare concrete. He knew that in a few weeks the place would be bustling with activity–children and adults running, splashing, laughing. For now, though, it was empty... quiet... lifeless.

As the days passed, he traveled further and further away from his house, away from the cave, out of his self-imposed hibernation. By the end of the week he walked far enough to be out of sight of his house. Again, there was anxiety and fear. At the same time, there was a sense of relief. It was as if some gigantic weight had been lifted from his shoulders. He knew he had a long way to go, many mountains to climb, many demons to battle. It would be a long journey, but for now, the daily walks were enough. It was a start. One step, one day at a time.

3 weeks later

Slowing his stride, Adam looked up and read the bright blue sign: Fenwick Hair Salon. Subconsciously, he ran a hand through his unruly hair. Realizing he was in desperate need of a haircut, he glanced to his right at the small strip of stores right up against the water. The hair salon sat in the middle of several shops that included a liquor store, sub shop and bakery. Shielding his eyes against the late morning sun, he saw the sign in the window: *Walk Ins Welcome*. He hesitated. As a few strands of hair blew across his face, he turned in that direction.

Entering the salon, he paused to let his eyes

adjust to the indoor lighting. Directly before him was a desk that held a small cash register and appointment book. The three styling chairs to his right were empty. Glancing around the room, his eyes were drawn to a glass-topped table. The obligatory hair styling magazines were scattered about. A vase of freshly cut flowers sat in the middle, their scent teasing the air.

Before any memories from the past were evoked, a voice called out. "May I help you?" Approaching him was a woman who looked to be in her early forties. Her Bohemian beach style dress complemented her tall thin body. Her shoulder length blond hair outlined her angular cheeks. Her face was smooth, her expression, welcoming. He could not help but stare. She was really quite attractive. Adam smiled–a rarity of late. "The sign says walk-ins are welcome."

She laughed–a pretty, gentle laugh. "Welcomed and most appreciated." She reached for a pencil. "Name?"

"Adam."

"Hello, Adam. I'm Melissa. Call me Mel."

"Hello, Mel." He was glad she didn't ask for his last name.

Entering his name in the appointment book, she dropped the pencil and motioned towards the first chair. Adam followed her direction. A short time later, he was staring at his face in a mirror. She was standing behind him, gently moving her fingers through his hair. "It's pretty long," she said.

"Yes it is."

"So, how do you want it cut?"

Adam hesitated. In the past he had always kept his hair cut short. "Just trim it up a bit."

"No problem. Come on over and let's get you shampooed."

He was tense at first, but slowly began to relax. She was pleasant and kept the conversation light. She talked about how slow the salon had been all winter, much of which she blamed on the economy and price of gas. She talked about how other businesses were feeling the crunch as well. She talked about the weather–today's forecast was for rain with a cold front extending into the weekend.

"Summer is just around the corner," Adam said, wanting to add at least something to the conversation.

"It can't come anytime too soon," she said. "Someone forgot to tell the electric company there was a recession going on."

Adam made no comment, instead sitting quietly with his eyes closed. Sensing his reluctance to talk, she started humming in a soothing melancholy tone. The song was familiar, but Adam could not recall the name. He focused on what she was doing with her hands. It felt good to have his head shampooed, his scalp messaged and to hear someone else's voice. It had been a long time since he had been so close to anyone. It had been a long time since he felt anyone's touch. It had been a long time for a lot of things.

When she was finished, she held up a mirror for him to inspect her work. Catching him looking at her instead, she gave him a wink. He blushed and looked away.

Paying at the cash register, he tried to think of something to say. The silence was broken as his stomach let out a growl.

"Sounds like you didn't have breakfast."

Adam forced a smile. "You're right."

Gesturing with the same hand holding his money, she said, "The place a few doors down has good bar food. They're noted for their wings. They have a band that plays there regularly, too," she added. "They play a little of everything, with a heavy flavor of country... *beach country* they call it. It's Friday, so they'll be there."

"Sounds interesting. Thanks."

"No problem." Her ever-present smile widened.

He returned the gesture as he headed out the door.

"Hey," she said. He stopped and looked over his shoulder. "Maybe I'll see you there sometime."

"Maybe," he replied.

*****

Outside, Adam looked up. When he started out earlier, the sky had been clear, the sun, bright. Now, black clouds had moved in. The smell of rain permeated the air. A clap of thunder caused him to look towards the south. It was even darker in that direction. While he wanted to finish his walk, he had no desire to get caught in the rain. He turned toward home–a good mile away. With each step, however, the storm drew closer. The wind picked up as well. It was obvious he wasn't going to make it home. Looking around for shelter, he saw the entrance to the bar. He made it through the doors just as the heavens opened.

He wiped a few drops from his face and looked around. He had entered in the middle of what appeared to be a long winding room. There was a wooden floor, a polished matching bar, mirrored walls and shelving that held a variety of spirits. Banks of beer taps were spread out like mile markers on a highway. The walls were covered with beer signs and other beach style decorations. Mixed in among all this were flat screen TVs of various sizes. In spite of the sensory overload, the place seemed to have a friendly atmosphere. Adam took the first seat he came to.

A bartender in his mid-thirties came over and wiped the area in front of Adam. He extended a hand and a wide smile. "Welcome to Smitty McGee's. I'm Bobby."

Adam hesitated before shaking hands. "Adam,"

he said.

"What can I get for you?" Bobby asked.

Adam hesitated again. "V.O. on the rocks."

The bartender returned with an overfilled glass of whisky. "Hungry?"

Adam nodded.

Bobby pulled a menu from beneath the counter. "Let me know if you have any questions," he said as he turned and walked away.

Adam pulled the glass towards him, the liquid threatening to spill over the side. He leaned forward and took a sip, then lifted the glass and took a larger swallow. The liquor teased his tongue before sliding down his throat, burning along the way. It had been over fourteen months since he had anything to drink. He just didn't have the desire; nor had there been the opportunity. The whisky tasted good. He took another swallow and looked outside. Rain smashed against the windows in waves. Lightning flashed. Claps of thunder followed. Yes, he had made it inside just in time.

Bobby returned, carrying a bottle of V.O. "So, what brings you to this neck of the woods?" he asked, refilling Adam's glass, again to a near overflowing level.

Adam shrugged the warning flags off. "Actually, I was walking by when the storm hit."

Bobby nodded. "Glad we could be of service."

"I was next door getting my hair cut."

"At Mel's?"

"I think that was her name."

"Tall, thin, blond. Nice tits."

Adam was a little taken aback at the specifics of the description. "Yes."

"Nice lady," Bobby said.

"She recommended I give you a try."

Bobby smiled and pointed to the menu. "We're known for our wings."

"She said that, too."

"Light, mild or spicy."

Remembering he had not eaten such food in a long time, Adam wisely chose mild.

Later, as he sat in front of his third drink and an empty basket of wings, Bobby came back to clear the dishes. "How were the wings?"

"Good... and hot," Adam said. His mouth was still burning.

Bobby smiled in agreement. "That they are. Another V.O.?"

Adam looked at his watch. "It isn't even one o'clock!"

Bobby laughed. "Long as you keep drinking, I'll keep pouring." The glass was refilled. "This one's on me."

Adam nodded. "Thanks." Silently, he told himself to take it easy. Again, it had been a long time since...

Bobby returned, wiping his hands on a towel tucked into his belt. "Dessert, coffee?"

"Coffee sounds good."

A cup of steaming coffee appeared, this time not filled to the rim. "Holler if you need anything." Adam had to smile. The bartender certainly moved fast.

Adam took advantage of the solitude, sipped his coffee and let his mind wander... wander into areas he had not visited in months. The anniversary of his wife's death had passed two weeks before–without fanfare, without responding to the many emails that day, without a visit to her grave. He simply spent the day alone in the beach house, sitting in his recliner, staring out the back at the vacant waterfront lots. It was quite a spectacular view for those interested in such things. But when he looked, he saw nothing. His body was numb. His mind was in an emotional coma. He spent most of his days that way until he took the first walk. Now, while still spending hours in the same chair, he took a daily stroll. The only hindrance was the weather.

He drained the last drop of liquor and did the same with the coffee. He turned and looked out the window. The storm was winding down. The sun was shining through parting clouds. He looked for Bobby to get the check. "One step at a time," he mouthed softly.

3

Mid-May

It was a quiet Thursday evening at Smitty McGee's. Adam sat in what had become his favorite area–right where the bar curved ninety degrees. From this vantage point, he could see in all directions. He wasn't sure why it was entertaining to sit at a bar and watch and listen to the people around him, but it was. He was careful, however, with his actions and his conversation. The last thing he wanted was to draw undue attention his way, even though Bobby seemed more and more interested in getting Adam's *story*, as the bartender liked to call it.

Glancing up, Adam saw Bobby heading in his direction. He was carrying two empty shot glasses and a bottle of B&B. Stopping in front of Adam, he filled the glasses. Sliding one towards Adam, he said, "You know Adam, you've been coming in here for what... a month now? But..." The B&B was downed and the empty glasses slid beneath the bar in case Sunny McGee, the owner, happened by. "We still don't know anything about you."

Adam chased the B&B with a sip of V.O. "Why is that so important?" he asked with a combination of curiosity and annoyance.

"It's not a matter of importance," Bobby said. "It's simply a matter of knowing your customers. Besides, I'm collecting material for a book I wanna write."

He didn't add that he pegged Adam early on as a very private person, which caused Bobby's level of curiosity to rise even more. Learning about his customers and finding out their story was how he passed the time behind the bar, which in spite of the apparent chaos at times, could be quite boring.

Adam's own curiosity overshadowed his annoyance. "A book... about what?"

"About the things I hear and see while I'm at work." Bobby leaned in closer and winked. "There's plenty of material if you pay attention."

Adam choked at having been caught at the same game. "Does this book have a title?" he asked as a way of recovery.

"*Behind Bars.*"

Adam's eyebrows rose. "Interesting name."

"I think so," the bartender said. "Anyway..."

"Anyway?"

Bobby smiled. "Who are you? What are you? What do you do?"

Adam hesitated and glanced at Mel, who was

absorbed in playing trivia on one of the TVs. He looked back at Bobby. "I guess you could say I'm a writer."

Bobby's eyes widened. "A writer... what do you write about?"

"Technical stuff... stuff most people wouldn't understand," Adam replied. "Some are journal articles. Some material is in book form." Adam had decided weeks before that if he had to give out any information about himself, this would be the direction he'd go. After all, it was the truth. He was extensively published.

"Cool," Bobby said. He started to walk away, then turned back around. "You know, you and I should write the book together."

"The book?"

"Yeah, *Behind Bars*."

Adam let out a laugh. It was his first genuine laugh in months.

"I'm serious," the bartender insisted. "It'd be fun."

"I don't know about that," Adam said. "I never considered writing fun."

"Then you're not writing about the right stuff."

Adam shrugged his shoulders. "I don't know," was all he could muster.

"Think about it," Bobby said. He waved his arms back and forth. "Besides..." He paused and gave Adam one of his signature smiles. "It writes itself."

The following Friday

It was the second night in a row the band *Beach House* played at Smitty's.

They were a local group who played the various bars and clubs in the area. While they played a lot of covers, much of their music was original, written by Ricky, the lead singer, during his early years in Nashville. Much of their sound was what Ricky liked to call beach country. It was the band that was playing the first night Adam went to Smitty's.

On this particular night, Ricky's voice was hoarse. He was making it, but barely, and had already broken off a couple of high notes. Mel leaned towards Adam and pulled a speck of lint off his shirt. She chuckled as Ricky broke yet another note. "He's really struggling tonight," she said.

"Why's that?" Adam asked, hoping there were more specks on his shirt.

"Because they play so much."

"How often do they play?"

"This time a year, two to three times a week. During the summer, they can play five...six days a week, sometimes more."
"Sounds like a lot," Adam acknowledged.

"It is. Anyway, I always told them they should make an album without any singing."

"Just music?" Adam sought to clarify.

The speck of lint removed, Mel's fingers gently massaged the area where the dust may have caused a bruise. It felt good to Adam. It also felt good to her. It had been a long time since she had touched anyone in such a fashion. It had been a long time since anyone had returned the favor. It had been a long time for a lot of things in her life. "Yeah, and I have a name for it, too," she said.

Adam leaned into her, giving positive reinforcement to her actions. "And?"

"*Duct Taped.*" With her free hand, she pulled an imaginary zipper across her lips.

Adam smiled. He closed his eyes and let his mind imagine what the band would sound like without the singing. There were other things he imagined as well.

Mel's imagination was on a roll, too.

*****

A loud smack ran through the air. All heads turned towards the far corner of the bar where a couple of ladies were in a heated discussion with Doug. Doug was one of the full-time bartenders who had worked at Smitty's since finishing college several years before. He was a tall muscular guy, well built with a head of curly blonde hair. Except for a weathered facial complexion and a crooked nose, the result of four years of West Virginia football, he wasn't bad looking–at least that's what the girls claimed. There was always an abundance of the female species in the section of the bar he was working. As far as work, Doug tended to do as much *bar talking* as bartending. But that criticism usually came from those not getting his undivided attention.

Anyway, the resonance of the hand slapping the bar cleared the air, the girl on the left–the older, prettier and much drunker one–said in a loud voice, "I do have a fucking grip on reality. I'm just not able to articulate it at the moment, that's all."

"Because you're drunk?" Doug said.

"Because I'm fuckin' *A* drunk."

Doug shook his head. "'m not sure if you'd have any better grip if you were sober."

The girl stared at him, obviously mad, and obviously trying to come up with an appropriate response. Before she could, Doug lit into her even more. "You know, the problem is that every time you break up with someone, you go into a deep depression, bemoaning about what might have been and badmouthing all the good there was. Well, sweetheart, let me tell you this, it takes two to tango, but only one to *untango*."

Now most people would have stopped here and given the girl a break–after all, she did just break up with her boyfriend of three years. But not

22

Doug the pontificator. He was on a mission. "Therein lies the problem," he continued. "Break-ups are seldom two partied. It's always one person dumping the other. Thus, one person always gets hurt. Unfortunately, you always seem to be on the short end of that stick." He paused a moment. "Let me ask you this, and be honest. Did you see this coming?"

The brokenhearted girl looked down. "Yes."

"I expected as much," Doug said. "Now..." He waited until she looked up. "The next time this happens... and believe you me, it will happen again... The next time, you put your offense in instead of your defense and you dump his mother-fucking-ass first." His voice dropped a few decibels. "Never give up control of the situation, even in a relationship." He paused and leaned forward. "You're a beautiful person, inside and out. Don't let anyone tell you otherwise."

A smile was born on the girl's face. Mission accomplished.

*****

Not long after his first visit to Smitty McGee's, Adam noticed a few things about the staff. They were all young, energetic and seemed to enjoy their jobs. For the most part, they worked well together. Of special note to Adam, and maybe an overused cliché, the female staff all had legs to die for. He'd been told Sunny was one of the best employers to work for. It spite of this, except for a handful who had been there for many years, the turnover of employees was high. Not only was there competition for customers, there was also competition for good staff, and good staff was hard to keep.

There was something else about the group as well. It wasn't until both Bobby and Doug stopped by together that Adam realized what it was. They all had weathered faces. Not necessarily a lot of wrinkles, not sunburn, but basically premature aging of the skin. As Doug and Bobby stood before him, all Adam could conjure up were two old salty sea captains. The only things missing were the caps and the cigars.

On the surface, the bar business appeared to be fun, but beneath the surface, there was a lot of stress... a lot of pressure to perform... to serve food... to push drinks. The bar business was cut-throat competition. It was the first time Adam realized just how sharp the knife was.

Not a whole lot different than modern day medicine, he surmised.

The door to the bar opened and three young things entered. The two sea captains turned and steered in their direction.

The competition was on.

*****

A quote from one of the patrons at the bar: "Everybody looks good naked... in the dark."

The following Friday

Adam certainly understood the concept of last call. He couldn't remember, however, ever participating in such a ritual. Anywhere from fifteen to thirty minutes before a bar stopped serving alcoholic beverages, an announcement was made in one form or another. The lights might be dimmed. The music might stop, or maybe even get louder. Or the bartenders would simply walk up and down announcing the event. Bobby claimed there was just something manly about closing down a bar–being one of the last to leave for the night. He liked to tell the tale of closing two bars in two states in one night. It sounded exotic, but in reality it wasn't all that big a deal. Delaware bars closed at 1:00 am, Maryland's at 2:00 am. You could leave any bar in Fenwick at 1:00 am and be in Maryland in five minutes. There were plenty of bars to choose.

A manly thing to do, Bobby claimed. Adam wondered how the women felt.

At Smitty McGee's, at approximately ten minutes before 1:00 all empty glasses or bottles were automatically refilled, and then the cash register printed out everyone's checks which were distributed appropriately. Bills were paid and tips slid across the bar. Some people up and left. Many, however, remained with the pretense of finishing their drink. It reality, at least according to Bobby, they didn't want to go out and face the world.

"It's a harsh world out there," Bobby said. "Many people have a hard time with that. Here, they can escape. It's like the land of lost souls." He didn't mention that he had Adam pegged in that category.

Tonight, Adam was living the ritual, living the fantasy. His glass had been topped off. The credit card receipt for the evening was sitting before him. He tried arguing silently that his own situation had nothing to do with all that. He arrived late, having taken an extra long nap earlier in the evening. His argument failed, however. He knew he was here escaping, just like the others around him. Since his emotional hibernation had ended and he had been going out more, the many truths he had been denying these months were percolating to the surface. Like ghosts in a graveyard, they were quite haunting. They were the same ghosts that had been with him the day he left his wife–to be buried in a cold steel coffin, alone, without her family, her many friends, without him, without anyone–just her and their unborn child.

To escape the ghosts, to escape the family and friends that swarmed around him like bees on a spring bed of clover, Adam drove to Fenwick the day of the funeral, cutting short his presence at the obligatory post-funeral reception. There, his hibernation began. There, he was able to bury the memories, his feelings, his pain. His mind and body were numb. His mind functioned at minimal capacity. He did just enough to survive. He had no death wish. Then again, he had no life wish either.

A year later, he started going for walks–around the house at first, then around the block, around the community, and then out past the safety net of his development. That was okay, he concluded. He bothered no one. No one bothered him. Then one day he ventured even further. He got a haircut. He went next door for lunch. He went back the same evening. Mel was there. They sat together. They talked–superficially, but they talked. She didn't ask any prying questions. He didn't offer any in-depth information. His hibernation was ending. At the same time, the pain he had been able to keep bottled up for so long was surfacing. The ghosts were returning. Now here he was, sitting at the bar at last call, not wanting to leave. He knew, however, he had to leave. He had to go out and face the world, the past, the memories, the demons–just like everyone else sitting around him.

But not just yet, he argued. He still had some of his drink left. He swirled the liquid around in the glass. He took a sip and swirled some more.

Bobby came up and asked, "You okay?"

Previous thoughts were buried. The demons went back into their box. "I'm fine," Adam said.

"You driving?"

"No, I walked."

"Want a cab?"

"Nah, the walk'll do me good." Adam hurriedly finished his drink and spun off the stool. "Later," he said as he headed for the door. Outside, the moon was half full. A few clouds slowly passed through the light. He took a deep breath. He was back in reality.

As he crossed Route 54 and headed towards home, part of him said he needed to go back into hibernation. He had been out long enough. The stress was starting to show. Another part told him he needed to stay on course. He'd be okay if he continued to watch what he said and what he did. Caution was key.

He nodded to himself. "Steady as she goes," he muttered. He ignored the warning of rough waters ahead.

4

Summer 2008
The first Sunday in June

Doug was on a roll again. This time he was arguing with a couple of middle aged men over the best location to watch baseball, more specifically Sunday Night Baseball. The game was about to start, and the two men were preparing to leave and go to another bar for the viewing. Doug, however, was trying to keep them in their seats. They'd been arguing for over ten minutes, spouting out various establishments around town with the pros and cons of each. Doug acknowledged the positives where appropriate and pointed out the negatives as well. However, he continued to maintain his position that the best place to watch baseball was at Smitty McGee's. The men told him he was full of shit. He in return told them they were all fucked up.

Adam, who was watching from across the way, wondered where in the customer service manual did it say this was the way to talk to someone who was about to leave a tip. Additional words were slung about, money was dropped on the bar, and the two men rose to their feet. One of the men said, "You can argue with the best of 'em, Doug, but you ain't said nothing yet that would convince me to stay here."

Doug looked down at the pile of money and then up at the two men. With a passion in his voice that only Doug could muster, he said, "Gentlemen, if sports are your religion, then Smitty McGee's is your cathedral."

The man looked at his copilot. The other man just smiled. At the same time, he reached over and gave Doug a closed fisted five. Then in unison, the two men slid back into their seats.

Adam, who had been watching this exchange from his perch at the bar, shook his head side to side as the conversation ended and the promo for Sunday Night Baseball began. When Bobby came by to refill his glass, he said, "He's something else, isn't he?"

Looking over his shoulder, the bartender replied, "Yeah, but don't take what you see in here as the real Doug."

"How's that?"

"It's like he's on the football field," Bobby said. "When he's here, most of the time he's loud and opinionated. Occasionally, he can turn on the charm. You never know what you're going to get from one minute to the next. When he's not working, he's very quiet, soft spoken and has a heart of gold. I've even heard the ladies call him a real teddy bear. The only exception is when he has his mother in here. Then he's on his best behavior the whole time."

Adam laughed. "Maybe you ought to bring his mother in here more often."

"Nah, who wants to see a teddy bear on a foot- . ball field?"

*****

The trivia phenomena that had been sweeping the country permeated the local bar scene as well. There were different names, different rules and different ways to play. The principle, however, was all the same–answer the question. At Smitty McGee's, the name of the game was Buzztime, and it was played by a lot of people nationwide. Questions came up on one of the TV screens. Answers were entered using a small blue computer box in front of the player. It was easy, fun and rather addicting.

There were different varieties, but the basic gist of the game was how fast you could answer a question. Points were awarded based on both correctness and speed of response. Bonus points were also available. While a customer only played against the other people in the same restaurant or bar, national rankings were shown every so often. One of the addictions was seeing your name up on the screen, knowing that people all over the country were looking at it. The game was played by people of both sexes and all ages, and while there was a sense of competition, there was also camaraderie amongst players–even when the locals were playing late at night for shots (low score buys).

Adam often watched from the sideline as a game progressed. Of interest was just how stupid he was compared to those who played for real– Mel included. He got the occasional question right, and there'd even be a run where he'd get two or three in a row correct, but if he played with the locals, he'd be buying a lot of shots.

In addition to the individual games, if you registered as an official Buzztime player, your score was accumulated over time. Those numbers and rankings were flashed up on the screen every so often as well. There were two players in the area who were in the top twenty-five nationally and were consistently the top two in the Delmarva region. The top player, Madcap, had over eighteen million points. Number two, Barracuda, had over twelve million.

An impressive score, Adam thought, until something very interesting struck him. Each game took approximately twenty minutes, with the maximum score, including potential bonus points, being around twenty thousand. The norm ran around twelve thousand. The math was rough, but the conclusion was valid.

Buzztime question: What does it take to earn eighteen million points?

Buzztime answer: A hell-of-a-lot of time at a bar!

Second Tuesday in June

It was unusual to hear Sunny McGee's voice when she was more than several feet away. Usually, she was rather soft spoken. Barely reaching five foot, she was as petite as she was short. She kept her dark brown hair in a pixie cut. She had a short stubby nose and dark green eyes. Eyeglasses, worn only to read small print, hung from one of those librarian type neck chains. While no one knew her true age–she had been claiming forty for several years–if you watched her in action, you'd realize she was an experienced restaurateur.

So when Adam heard her voice and saw she was a good distance away, his ears perked up. It was mid-week with an hour before closing. Sunny was standing in front of a middle aged woman who seemed to be alone. The woman had short cropped brunette hair, a round face that showed signs of make up running down her cheeks and a painful expression. Sunny was standing on a small stool, so she was eye level with the woman as she spoke. "Besides all that, you've been through this before. How long have I known you... since high school, right?" The bar owner didn't wait for an answer. "Right! And how many boyfriends have you had during that time? Five... six if you count that dickhead who was married. And each time it's the same thing. They steal your soul, break your heart and you end up in here all cried up and pissed off at the world. Well, sweetheart, as I've told you before, men are dicks, and should only be used for the same. Once you get that through that thick skull of yours, you'll be much better off." She handed the woman a Kleenex and reached over and gave her a hug. The woman looked up and forced a smile. The tears looked like they were starting to subside.

Bobby, who wisely remained at the other end of the bar during this conversation, strolled over to Adam. "Don't know that I've ever heard her talk like that before," Adam said.

Bobby nodded in agreement. "There's little in life that gets Sunny riled up, but men breaking the hearts of women is one of them."

"How do you know it's always the man's fault?"

Bobby leaned in and spoke quietly. "Where are you right now?"

Adam shrugged his shoulders. "At Smitty McGee's."

"And who owns Smitty McGee's?"

Adam pointed toward Sunny. "Sunny McGee, there."

Bobby leaned in closer. "Exactly. Rule number one, when you're at Smitty McGee's, the man is always wrong."

*****

Two old men were sitting next to one another, each nursing a draft. They were watching with interest as Sunny prepared drinks for a couple of young ladies who had just arrived. One old man leaned over to the other as if to whisper, but actually spoke in a loud enough voice for all to hear. "When did cranberry juice become the staple of a drink?"

Both men just shook their heads and continued sipping their beers.

*****

For whatever reasons, Adam was finding himself more and more relaxed as he started to enjoy his visits to the bar. As his comfort level grew, so did his *people watching*. It was an amazing group of humanity that came to Smitty McGee's. Diversity was a fair description. Who were they? What were they? Where did they come from? Why did they come here? In short, as Bobby liked to say, what were their stories? They did have one thing in common, however. They acted like a flock of honey bees. They went out. They worked. When work was over, they came back to the hive, deposited their honey, and in return were rewarded with a cold mug of mother's milk. *The Bee Hive.* That would be an interesting name for a bar, Adam thought.

Why, Adam thought. Why did people come to Smitty's, or any other bar for that matter? There were certainly plenty to choose from in the area. It was a question that haunted him nightly. After several months, Adam thought he had the answer. It was camaraderie without commitment. You could make barfriends, get close to them and yet have no obligation to them outside the arena.

Besides, there was divergent entertainment at the ready–music, trivia and sports. But for the most part, it was the camaraderie.

As Adam took a sip of his drink, Mel leaned in a little closer. Her free hand went up to the back of his neck and rubbed it gently. Her touch felt good. It felt relaxing. It felt supportive. He looked over at her. She looked at him, but only for a moment before her eyes returned to the Buzztime screen and the fierce battle among her and several other patrons. Adam smiled. Was she a worker bee or a queen bee? Were they barfriends or was there something more?

His thoughts were interrupted as Bobby buzzed

by, a bottle of VO in one hand, two shots of B&B in the other. Setting the glasses down, he said, "Did I tell you how hung over I am tonight?"

Adam laughed. "No Bobby, you did not."

"Well, I'm so fucking hung over, it ain't funny."

"Why are you hung over?" Adam asked innocently enough.

Bobby cocked his head to the side. "You really ask some stupid questions at times." With that, he gave Adam one of his wide smiles. He raised his glass of B&B. "Cheers."

"Cheers," Adam said aloud. To himself, he added, "Mother's milk." He followed the B&B with a swallow of whisky.

"Training wheels," Bobby said, pointing to the V.O.

"Huh?"

"If you have to drink something with your shot, it's called training wheels."

Adam laughed. "Can't say I ever heard that before."

"I'm sure there are a lot of things in here you haven't heard. That's why we should write a book."

Adam shook his head side to side as Bobby collected the empty glasses and turned to walk away. Adam put his thoughts to words. "Hey Bobby, what's *your* story?"

A half-smile crossed the bartender's face. "You wouldn't believe me if I told you."

Adam tipped his head to the side. "I could say the same thing."

"I doubt that," Bobby said, shrugging his shoulders. "I've seen and heard it all. You may get a raised eyebrow, but that's about it."

Ignoring the caution flags flapping wildly, Adam said, "What would you say if I told you I was a world famous pediatric neurosurgeon who traveled the world drilling holes in the skulls of little guys?"

As promised, Bobby's eyebrows did rise. The previous smile widened. "I'd say you were full of shit."

Adam stared at the bartender. "You a betting man, Bobby?"

"Occasionally."

Caution flags continued to flap wildly. "How about a bottle of B&B?"

"Exactly what are we betting on?" Bobby inquired.

"Whether I am or am not full of crap."

Bobby laughed. "You're on there, old man." He turned and walked away.

Without taking her eyes off the TV screen, Mel leaned over and said, "Why are you taking the boy's money like that?"

Adam's head snapped in her direction. He said nothing. He looked up at the TV. The game winner was being announced. It was Mel.

*****

Bobby took a sip of coffee followed by a bite of the cold burger the kitchen made for him an hour before. He was hungry enough, however, it didn't matter. When he first started in the bar business, he despised eating cold food. Food was something you took your time with. Even when he was a cop in his earlier days, you took time to eat. While it may not have fallen in the category of healthy, the food was always hot and eaten slowly. The bar business, however, was something entirely different. Here, you ate when you could, and as fast as you could. It was said the surest way to fill empty seats was to order food for yourself. Bobby smiled at the idea. If it was only that easy.

Another bite, another mouthful of coffee and the hunger pains started to subside. He was sitting in what they called the war room–a small cramped closet-like space stuck in the far corner of the building. The wall was lined with tables and chairs, with a calculator and pad sitting on each table. Besides serving as the break room, it was where the bartenders and wait staff reconciled their register drawers and tips at the end of their shift. Discrepancies had to be rechecked, and if still there, were logged in separately. Shortages came out of the tip bucket. Overages were put in an old pickle jar that sat up on the shelf–money for Sunny's Christmas present. The year before they collected enough to buy her a gold necklace with the letters SMG engraved on a heart-shaped disk. Bobby had yet to see her without it.

It always amazed Bobby that even on a super busy night with several bartenders working out of the same drawer, the numbers were usually close. Bartenders may sneak a drink here and there, and pass one on to a customer now and again, but they were honest with the money. Luckily tonight, everything tallied to within thirty-seven cents, which he didn't even worry about as he added the difference from his own pocket. Looking over his shoulder to make sure no one else was watching, he added a couple extra dollars to the pickle jar above. He then added the cash drawer and the credit cards together. It had been a good night... not a great one, but no one would bicker too much.

The last thing was to put rubber bands around the credit card receipts and then load up the night deposit bag. But there he stopped. He flicked the edges of the papers much like he would a deck of cards. Hesitating, he unwrapped the receipts and quickly looked through them. Finding the one he wanted, he pulled it out and laid it on the table. Squinting as the ink in the printer ribbon was inevitably low, he wrote the information on a piece of scrap paper. He put the

receipt back in the pile and stuffed everything into the money bag just as Doug came strolling in.

"How'd we do?" Doug asked.

Bobby knew it was a rhetorical question because Doug had an amazing mind for numbers.
He could guesstimate how much they made on
any given night without tallying up the receipts,
and be pretty darn close. Bobby slid the pad of
paper containing the nightly numbers around for
his coworker to see. At the same time, his other
hand palmed the piece of scrap paper.

"Not bad," Doug said. "About what I figured."

"What say we go over to Nick's for a nightcap?"
Bobby said. Nick's was a restaurant and bar in
Ocean City that was a late night rendezvous point
popular with the locals.

Doug nodded. "I'll see if anybody else wants to
go."

"I'll finish up here," Bobby said. He did just
that which also included stuffing the scrap paper
into his pocket.

Thursday afternoon

Bobby watched Adam head out across the parking lot. The bartender shook his head side to side.
A strange dude, he thought. Then he corrected
himself. Not strange, just mysterious. He turned
as he heard his name called. One of the new food

runners was standing a few feet from him. She was young, cute and trying hard, so he smiled and took the tray from her. He didn't know her name; then again, why bother? The staff turnover was so high, she'd be gone before he knew it. He served the food to a group of golfers who had come in earlier. They were thirsty and hungry, just the way he liked them.

The next hour passed quickly. Then, as so often happened in the middle of the afternoon, the place died. It was what they called a *dead bar*–not one customer in the entire place. Anticipating as much, he had already put in his lunch order. Maybe he'd get a relaxing meal today. Grabbing his chicken salad on rye off the food line, he headed for Sunny's office.

The office was small, dark, without windows and had piles of paper everywhere. There was an old metal desk, a non-descript wooden chair and a side table that contained a computer and printer. He paused as he entered the room. There was an immediate sense of confinement–a feeling generated from knowing the room had once been a bank vault. He sat down at the desk, took a bite of food and turned towards the computer. Closing out the screen saver, he opened the Internet and went to the Google home page. Unfolding the scrap paper from the night before, he looked at it before typing in *Adam Singer*. He quickly hit the search button before he changed his mind. Multiple pages of names appeared. He added the middle initial which narrowed the list to one page. He added Delaware to the search criteria. The search came up empty. He paused before changing Delaware to Maryland. This time three names appeared. Two were MySpace referrals. Doubting Adam would be a MySpace user, he opened the third.

A moment later, his jaw dropped nearly to the desk. "Son-of-a-bitch!" he said aloud.

*****

Adam overheard a woman at the bar one night say she wanted a wife... someone who could go to Walmart for her and take care of the kids. Her female companion for the evening said that she wanted the same. She also wanted someone who could sleep with her husband.

Friday evening

Bobby watched Adam come through the door and head towards his favorite area of the bar. He slid up on an empty stool and leaned forward. As most customers did when they entered a bar, Adam looked around to see what was going on. It was early yet. The dinner crowd had faded and the evening bar crowd had yet to arrive. It was

43

Behind Bars

still an hour before *Beach House* was scheduled to start.

The bartender grabbed a clean glass, filled it with ice and headed toward the newest customer. On the way, he grabbed a package from beneath the bar.

"Evening," Adam said. He watched as a paper bag was set before him. "What's that?"

"Open it," Bobby directed, filling the glass with whisky.

Taking a sip of his drink, Adam looked into the bag. He pulled out a bottle of B&B. "What's this?"

Bobby looked around to make sure no one was paying him any attention. "You're a fucking world famous brain surgeon... just like you said!"

"Pediatric neurosurgeon," Adam corrected.

"Whatever. On top of that, you've written books, and hundreds of magazine articles as well."

"Journal articles," Adam again corrected.

"Whatever." Bobby continued to stare at the customer. "I only have one question, Adam... Dr. Singer. What the fuck are you doing down here?"

Adam's mouth opened and closed. His head dropped down. A wave of sadness engulfed him. He always wondered how long he could stay incognito. He figured as long as he kept to himself, ventured out as little as possible, and otherwise stayed in the house, he'd be okay. But he hadn't done that, had he? He cursed himself for being so

44

stupid... so careless. To even think he could remain hidden from the world, from reality, from the memories. He should have known better!

He looked up at Bobby. Their eyes met. The bartender leaned forward. "I asked you a question. That doesn't mean you have to answer it. When you're ready to talk, I'll be ready to listen." He stepped away and returned with two shots of B&B. Sliding one forward, he lifted his own. "Here's to our secret... Doc." A thin smile crossed his face. "Cheers."

Adam clicked glasses and drank the liquid quickly. He chased it with a big swig of V.O. "Training wheels," he said aloud. "Like we said before, I'll tell you my story when you tell me yours."

Bobby returned the smiled. "Fair enough." Collecting the empty glasses, the bartender turned and strutted away.

5

From Doug the bartender: We all wallow at times in a jail cell of self-pity.

*****

A conversation Adam overheard one night between several middle aged women. One was telling the story of how she was jogging along Route 20 earlier that day when a big old billy goat came up to her. She stopped to pet the goat when it started to attack by bending his head down and trying to ram her with his horns. "They were big horns, too," she said.

"What did you do?" one woman asked.

"I grabbed it by the horns and wrestled with the old thing for at least twenty minutes. Finally, someone came by on a bicycle and chased it away. Man, was I relieved. Who knows what could have happened!"

One of the other women in the group laughed and said, "Why, all 'ole Billy wanted was to make love to you. You should have done it, and then he would have gone to sleep. You could have finished your run without a problem. Besides, a goat lasts less than a minute."

"How in the hell do you know that?" someone else piped in.

"Why, I run along that road every day," the woman spouted.

Sunday night

There are a lot of things that make a particular bar popular–that set it apart from the competition. Depending on the particular establishment, there are a lot of words that could be used to describe this phenomenon. The one that Adam felt best fit Smitty McGee's was *character*. Like a Disney attraction, not only did the place have character, it was also full of characters. The most famous characters were the people who worked there. There were also the customers who added a thrill to the attraction. Some of the customers were *newbies*, some regulars, some steady but not so regular. Then there were those that made a guest appearance: they came in once and were never seen again.

A lad named Donny Goldberg–they called him Donny G–fit into the steady but not so regular category. Adam had seen him two, maybe three times over the past couple months. It was reported that he was twenty-eight years of age, but he looked to be nary a day over eighteen. He was short, with a head of closely cropped hair. He had big ears, the kind that seemed to bend forward for better hearing. His nose was flat and his teeth were straight, although his teeth were seldom shown in a smile. His eyes were dark, almost jet black, and never seemed still. His neck was wide with veins protruding like vines crawling up a wall. The rest of his body... well the rest of his body was just plain skinny.

Donny G always came into the bar with a couple of other fellows, usually much bigger and stronger looking. They would take their seats, drink their beers and watch the TVs. Sometimes they played trivia, sometimes not. They always ate enough for themselves as well as several others. Wings–the hotter the better–was their favorite. Donny G wasn't one to smile a lot, but he was always friendly, introducing his buddies to Bobby, and to Sunny if she was around. It was obvious Donny G and Bobby went way back as there was always a hug thrown in with the usual handshake. In addition, Donny G's presence added an even brighter smile to Bobby's face and an extra pop to his stride.

As an object of people watching, Adam began to wonder about Donny G. Who was he? What did he do for a living? What was his story? The same questions he was reluctant to answer himself.

Adam decided Donny G was in the construction

business. He was probably the owner of the company, or at least a foreman. The guys he brought in were the people who worked with him. So that was the story Adam concluded, and he pretty much convinced himself he was correct, too. That is until Bobby stopped by with a refill. "Donny G there is one of my best and oldest friends. I'm always glad to see him walk through the door, cause that means he survived another mission."

"Another mission?" Adam said, confused with what a mission had to do with the construction business.

"Yeah, he doesn't talk about it much, and only a few of his closest friends know, but he's a Lieutenant in the Army Special Forces. Never know it by looking at him, would you? When he comes home, he usually brings along a couple of the guys who were on the mission with him. If you watch them closely, the first thing they do is toast the success of the mission. The second thing is a toast to anyone who may not have made it back." Adam's eyes widened at the comment. Bobby continued. "Yes, dear Adam, that happens a lot more than Joe Public ever knows. Special Forces don't get a whole lot of attention–dead or alive." Bobby took a deep breath. "Anyway, he disappears for days, sometimes weeks at a time. Where he goes or what he does, he's not allowed to say. But I will tell you this..." The bartender looked in both directions to make sure their conversation remained private. "There's no one better in the whole U.S. Army with a rifle at a thousand yards than Donny G. I've heard he could easily win an Olympic gold medal, if he was allowed to compete." Another pause, another glance in Donny G's direction. "Yeah, I'm always glad to see him walk through the door." Bobby nodded and headed off to refill the glass of his friend.

Adam just stared. What happened to the construction foreman who was having a couple beers with his coworkers after a hard day's work? Adam stared a few more seconds. Donny G, a true blooded American character all right. Not quite in the mold of Disney, but a character none the less.

*****

One bar patron to the other. "Why does a gentleman always let a lady go first?"

"I don't know. Why?" his buddy said.

"Because he doesn't have eyes in the back of his head."

"That's a dumb one," said the buddy. They each took sips of their beer and watched as Sunny stopped a few feet away and pulled a beer out of the cooler for herself. She nodded at the men as she carefully wrapped the bottle in a cocktail napkin and rubber band.

"I'll give you one," the buddy said once the

owner was out of earshot. "Why does Sunny always do that?"

"Do what?" the first man asked.

"Look at her. She always wraps her beer in a cocktail napkin."

"Fuck if I know. Ask her, you dumb shit."

"You ask her."

"Hey, I'm not the dumb one."

Early July 2008

As his people watching skills progressed, Adam found himself spending more and more time practicing the same. On one particular evening, he noticed a young to middle aged woman sitting alone at the corner of the bar. She wasn't knockout gorgeous, but she was pretty in her own right. She had long black hair, a thin narrow face and lips that were covered in a deep red shade of lipstick. She wore a purple tank top and pair of designer jeans. She sat quietly, watching and listening to the music. Her facial expression held a faint hint of a smile. Her right leg was crossed over the left and moved up and down in time with the music. Neither her position nor her expression changed for many minutes. For whatever reason, she struck a curious nerve in Adam. There was something intriguing about her, something mysterious. Who was she? What was she?

Why was she here, and alone no less? In short, what was her story?

Just as his curiosity was rising, she grabbed her cell phone off the bar and went outside. Adam watched her pace back and forth, one hand pressing the cell phone to her ear, the other hand at her side. Adam couldn't tell whether she was smoking a cigarette or not. He couldn't see any, but decided she probably was. A woman who smoked was much more mysterious to Adam than one who didn't. This activity continued until the end of the song when she strolled in, retook her seat and assumed the previous position, all the while acting as if nothing had happened. The question of her story again crossed Adam's mind.

He took a nervous look around the bar and wondered just how many people were wondering the same thing about him?

A short time later, Adam found himself watching an elderly couple across from him. They sat close together. They seemed to have eyes only for each other. Each had a draft and they were sharing a piece of pie. She looked healthy enough for her age. He looked downright ill. *Skin and bones* was being polite. A closer look showed he had a tracheostomy, which he covered with a finger every time he wanted to talk.

It was a sight to see. A wave of happiness passed through Adam–happiness for the couple across from him. After all these years, they were still very much in love. It brought true meaning to the concept: in sickness and in health.

Adam tried to cut the thought off as he remembered the rest of the wedding vow. It was too late, however. The words were already on the tip of his tongue. Till death do we part. The wave of happiness was replaced by one of sadness. Why couldn't he and Nancy be sitting here now, drinking a beer, sharing a piece of pie?

Yes, it was a sight to see. It was a tough pill to swallow. It was also another story to tell.

6

Late July

"Do you know how hard... how incredibly hard it is to write a book?" Adam asked, a hint of exasperation in his voice. They had been at it for several minutes, Bobby insisting they could do it; Adam arguing to the contrary. "You not only have to put words down on paper, you have to do it in an organized, intelligent fashion, and always in a way to keep your reader's interest. You also have to go at it with the attitude that the reader is giving you his valuable time–time you should not waste with run on sentences, useless words, and things like that. Then, when you think you have it right, you have to go over each word again and again–cutting, pasting and more cutting. It can be a gut wrenching experience. You struggle with sentence structure, paragraph breaks... even punctuation."

"Punctuation?" Bobby interrupted.

"Yeah, punctuation... like commas."

"What's so special about commas?" Bobby asked.

"You get in more arguments with your editor

and coauthors over commas than anything else. I call it playing chicken with commas."

"I like to play chicken," Bobby said. "Only I use a gun."

Adam laughed. "I can see this is going to be tough."

"Maybe... maybe not," Bobby said without the laugh. "It all depends on how many eggs the chicken lays."

Adam tilted his head to the side. "That doesn't make any sense, Bobby."

"Makes about as much sense as arguing over a damn comma! Anyway, who gives a fuck where the commas go? It's about the words surrounding them that are important, right?"

Adam could only stare. Finally, "It's a daunting task, to say the least."

"And becoming a doctor was easy?" Bobby countered.

"Yes... no... but..."

"Ain't no commas in that sentence, are there?" Bobby turned and walked away.

He strutted down to where two new customers were just getting adjusted on their respective bar stools. They told Bobby their drink of choice which told anyone nearby they were newbies. Unless your choice of beverage was inconsistent, you only had to order once from Bobby the bartender. He could spot an empty glass a mile away. He had eyes like a hawk and the memory of a... the memory of a...

Yes, it's hard writing a book. Sometimes you struggle for hours just to find the right word, and then you still can't come up with it.

*****

During a short break in the music from *Beach House,* a young lady well on her way to being intoxicated leaned over to Adam and put her arm around his shoulder. In a slurred speech, she said, "Feel free to give me your number and I'll decide if I want to call you or not." She straightened up, winked at him and laughed. Her attention returned to her friends sitting on her other side.

Bobby came by a few minutes later. Adam leaned in and quietly said, "I was just propositioned by the girl sitting beside me."

Bobby laughed and nodded to the girl in question. "Don't feel too special. She asks everybody for their number."

"She's young enough to be my daughter," Adam said.

Bobby laughed again. "It's a strange world in here sometimes, I'll tell you that."

The music restarted. Ricky sang, "You gotta love that..."

When the next song ended, there was the normal generous round of applause. Ricky adjusted the guitar strap around his neck and stepped closer to the mike. "Hey Bobby," he said. "We're thirsty." He held up an empty bottle of beer.

Adam looked at the windowsill behind the band. It was already full of empty bottles with shot glasses intermingled among the tall necks. Adam shook his head and said, "How do they drink so much and still stay standing?"

"They're professional drinkers," a man standing beside him said.

A round of shots provided by someone at the bar came along with the beer. Ricky set the beer down and held up his shot glass. Others in the band followed. "The demons of liquor," he said. He took a sip to wet his lips. "Can I get an amen?"

"Amen," the crowd said.

"Can I get another?"

The crowd responded even louder. "Amen!"

Ricky held his glass higher. "The gospel according to Jim Beam." In unison, the glasses were emptied. Ricky sat his on the ledge with the other empty glasses, readjusted the guitar and said, "We're *Beach House,* otherwise known as the *Bourbon Tabernacle Choir.* Welcome to Smitty McGee's."

The drummer started the beat for the next song. Adam glanced over at his unsolicited admirer. She now had her arms draped around another gentleman sitting a few stools down. She was whispering something in his ear. Adam smiled. It was a strange world all right.

7

From Doug the bartender: Never underestimate the insanity beneath the surface of a sane appearing man, and never underestimate the sanity below the surface of one who acts insane.

*****

People watching was not a new activity for Adam. As a physician, he watched patients and families, especially when doing a history and physical. The purpose was to get as much information as possible regarding the patient's illness. And because he dealt with pediatrics and because it was his nature in general, he often got into their personal lives. The difference was that outside of medicine, he had no definitive impact on the people he watched or interacted with. In medicine, however, his skill level could be a deciding factor in the rest of a child's life.

On this particular night, he'd been observing a couple sitting near the head of the bar directly in front of the band area. They were an older couple, he looked to be in his fifties, she at least her forties. He was tall, thin and weathered looking. She was what one might call a pretty Plain Jane. She was much shorter than he. He wore a John Deere hat and a green sweatshirt advertising some other piece of farm equipment. He had the look of a working man, and Adam had little doubt it was more than a look. He wore a pair of old jeans and a pair of just as worn work boots. She was more dressed up. Her hair, shoulder length, was curled and swung gently back and forth as she nodded her head in time to the music as Beach House was in full swing. She wore a plain, yet pretty, white sweater that more than adequately showed off her well-proportioned figure. There was a small pair of dangling earrings and a sparse amount of makeup. Her sweater was short sleeved, so you could see her arms. She too had the muscle mass of a working girl. Her waist and below were covered in a pair of much newer jeans, white socks and clean tennis shoes.

They had been there ever since Adam had arrived an hour before. They sat quietly in their places, each sipping beer from a bottle and listening to the music. A plate of nachos sat between them which they addressed every so often.

Bobby stopped by and said, "What are you watching so intently?"

Adam turned around with an *I just got caught with my hand in the cookie jar expression* on his face. "Nothing," he stammered.

"Bullshit," Bobby contested.

Adam laughed. "I was just looking at that couple over there." He motioned in the appropriate direction.

Bobby looked in the appropriate direction as well. "Oh, that's Charlie and his old lady. You'd never know it by looking at 'em, but he's one of the richest men around here."

"How's that?"

"Owns the biggest farm in Delmarva... several thousand acres. Raises chickens and corn mostly, but dabbles in cattle as well. His wife, she works the garden–big ass garden, too. Plants several hundred acres just in produce. Brings Sunny tomatoes and corn once in a while. Best damn corn you'll ever taste, too." Bobby paused and wet his whistle from a bottle of Coke. "They come in here most Fridays. Three beers each, a plate of nachos and a five dollar tip. Never anything less, never anything more."

Adam shrugged his shoulders. "No problem with that, I guess."

"You'll never hear me complain about a consistent customer," Bobby said. "That's the foundation of what keeps a place like this alive. We couldn't make it just on the tourist trade. It's becoming a problem. Ocean City and Fenwick are both chasing the locals away."

"How's that?"

"The price of real estate. People who work here

can't afford to live here anymore. A sad state of affairs, and it's only going to get worse."

"Do locals have that big an impact on the economy?"

"Like I said, they keep us alive, especially in the off season." Bobby nodded and headed toward some empty glasses. He was back a few minutes later, two shots of B&B in one hand, a plate of cheesy fries in the other. Setting everything down, he took a fry for himself. "The kitchen made a mistake, or so it would appear."

"Would appear?" Adam said through a mouth of potatoes. He was also sucking in air hard as they were mighty hot.

Bobby smiled. "My screw up."

"Does it come out of your hide?"

"We drink for free. We don't eat for free."

Adam was more careful with the next bite. "Then put these on my tab."

"That's mighty kind of you, but my screw up, my skin." He looked down to where Charlie and his wife were still sitting at the bar, only now they were on their third and final beer. "Yeah, ole Charlie there's something else. In his day–that is before Jane got her claws in him–he was a wild one. He and Sunny went to school together, and some of the stories she tells–nothing bad, just wild. More than three beers is all I'll say."

"His wife have that much influence on him?" Adam asked, watching the couple as well.

"That and the fact that his liver is failing him a might. Besides, he has two daughters to look after, and he does that with an iron fist... or so he thinks. They come in here once in a while. And I'll tell you this, they certainly live up to the reputation that farm girls are hot and horny."

"Personal experience?"

Bobby laughed. "What happens on the farm stays on the farm."

He moved away and Adam continued watching the couple in question. He kept his glances casual, looking at the band and other people as well. Yet, his focus of attention remained on the Charlie and Jane show. Now Charlie was standing at Jane's side, his chest up against her shoulder. One hand held his beer; the other was around her back, his fingers gently pulling at the material of her sweater. She did not seem to mind the attention as her free hand was also around his back–doing what, Adam could not see. There was little doubt by looking at their features, they lived a hard life. There was little doubt by listening to Bobby, that like a wild horse, Charlie had been tamed by the cowgirl at his side. There was little doubt they had raised a fine family; and in spite of the many years they had been together, they were still in love with each other and the life they led.

Adam felt happy for them, sad for himself. He turned away as his eyes began to water. In love with each other... Oh, how he missed Nancy.

He felt an arm atop his shoulder. He looked to his right. Mel, eyes fixed on the screen in front of her, gave him a gentle squeeze. She started to pull her hand away, but he reached up and grabbed it. "That feels good," he said softly.

She looked at him and smiled. "Thank you," he mouthed, smiling back.

She nodded and returned to her game.

He returned to his game as well–people watching.

*****

Speaking of people watching, Adam noticed an older lady who had made her way onto the dance floor. She was gyrating (if that's what you called it) with a couple of young bucks. She was dressed in a tight red top and tight jeans. She wore glasses, long dangling earrings and had her hair in a bouffant. She had one of those thin gold bracelets around her left ankle. She was barefooted, and then Adam saw them! "She's got bunions, for God's sake," he muttered to the wind.

*****

Another interesting phenomenon Adam noticed since honing his observation skills was the change in the dress code for bars and restaurants. It certainly wasn't what he'd been accustomed to as a child when you came off the beach in the afternoon and dressed up for dinner. In today's world, people may get cleaned and dressed for dinner. They certainly, however, didn't get dressed up. Bobby referred to it as F.G.W.–fashion gone wild.

*****

Staying on the subject of fashion, except for the long ponytail wrapped in numerous rubber bands, except for the tattoos up and down both arms, except for the black shirt with bright white lettering across the back telling all you can do on a Harley, except for the diamond studded earring protruding from one earlobe, except for the tight black jeans held up by a heavy leather belt, the guy across from the bar looked just like Adam.

It was Wednesday–biker's night.

And a good time was had by all… even Adam, who watched in amazement as bikers poured in–male and female–and acted like normal human beings.

*****

It was obviously a bachelorette party as a group

of seven or so young to middle aged women were gathered at the far end of the bar. They'd been there for most of the evening and had consumed a fair amount of alcohol. The girls were rowdy early on, but as was often the case at such an event, the reality of the next couple days started to override the effects of the booze. One of their own was leaving the coop, and they were all sad.

One girl (assumed to be the maid of honor) asked the drunkest girl (obviously the bride-to-be) if she had any last requests.

The bride-to-be brushed a wad of hair from her face. She looked up and down the bar and found the target of her attention. She pointed in that direction. "Him," she said loudly.

All eyes (including the casual observers around the party) followed the line of sight. She was pointing directly at Bobby the bartender.

August 2008

While the place didn't seem all that noisy for an early Friday evening, it was still crowded. As such, Adam jumped on the first unoccupied bar stool he saw. Seeing him, Sunny broke off the conversation she was having with a couple of men dressed in polo shirts and long pants sitting a couple seats down. Sliding a cocktail napkin toward him, she said, "V.O.?"

"Please," Adam said.

Adam watched as Sunny filled the glass with ice followed by the whisky. Adam immediately noticed the glass wasn't overflowing. "Thanks," he said with a grin.

"No problem. How are you tonight?" Sunny countered.

"I'm okay. I had a nice walk today."

"And now you're thirsty," Sunny chuckled.

"And hungry."

"Wanna see a menu?"

"In a bit."

Sunny nodded and started to redirect her attention back to the two men. She halted her action, however, and turned back to Adam. "Hey, Adam. You seem like a smart man. Maybe you have an idea." Before she went any further, she introduced him to the other two men. Both were Fenwick Island City Councilmen. Handshakes were exchanged as were smiles. They weren't as wide as the infamous Bobby the bartender's smile, but they were big nonetheless.

"Anyway," Sunny continued, "We've been lamenting about the fact that Ocean City gets all the attention and we get nothing."

"Attention in what way?" Adam inquired, taking the first sip of his drink.

"As a fun place for people to go... to go eat and drink that is."

"Isn't that what Fenwick Island wants? To be

69

thought of as the quiet place?" Adam asked.

"As far as the hustle-bustle is concerned, yes," one of the councilmen replied. "But we still want the business."

"Just not the riff-raff," the other councilmen said.

"So basically, you're looking for ways to show-case your businesses."

"Exactly," both councilmen said in unison. "We're mainly looking at the food and beverage industry though," Sunny injected. "Least that's what we're talking about here."

"I see," Adam said. He sipped his drink. What the hell did he know about the bar business, he wondered silently. A blast of warm air came in as the door nearest them was driven open by several men, each wearing shorts, tee shirts and hats. The look in their eyes told even the casual observer that they were thirsty. The sunburn on their faces answered the question of why. If one still needed a clue, each sported a logo on the back of his shirt promoting the White Marlin Open. It was one of the largest fishing tournaments on the east coast, and brought millions into the economy of Ocean City. And the town of Fenwick wanted a piece of the action. Nothing wrong with that, Adam concluded as he watched Bobby serve up drafts to the men who just arrived. "The White Marlin Open is this weekend, huh?" he said.

"Actually, it goes on all week," one of the councilmen said.

"What goes on next weekend?" Adam asked.

The two men and Sunny hesitated. "Nothing that I know of," Sunny said.

At that moment, Adam noticed a bottle of Kahlua sitting on the counter. It triggered one of those instant cerebral pop-ups that happens every so often. "Then have your own open," he said. Before anyone could argue, he explained. "Call it the White Russian Open–Fenwick Island's first annual bar tour."

"A bar tour?" the first councilman said with a blank stare.

"A bar tour!" said the other.

The two councilmen were now looking at one another, wide smiles forming on their faces. "We did that at college my senior year," one said.

"I think a lot of universities do at the end of the school year," Sunny said.

"Then, Fenwick University here we come," said the other.

As a thank you, Sunny gave Adam a wink and a pinch on the cheek. "You know Adam, for someone who drinks whisky, you're really a smart guy," she teased. She capped off his drink. This time, the glass did overflow.

*****

"Well, good morning," Mel said with a bright smile as Adam walked through the door of the salon. "Did you get home okay last night?"

Adam returned the smile, albeit a bit meekly. He had to admit having more than usual to drink the night before. It seemed he along with several other patrons, including the two councilmen, started the bar tour a week early. "No problem," he said. "You?"

Mel laughed. "Two glasses of wine over three hours. If can't handle that, maybe I should go to the library instead of the bar."

Adam continued his smile. "I'm glad you had a good time."

"So, how can I help you?" Mel inquired.

Adam looked around. There was one elderly lady under the hairdryer, otherwise the salon was empty. "Walk-ins still welcome?"

Mel laughed again. "Sure, come on in. I think I know how you want it cut. Let's go ahead and get you shampooed." When she was finished washing his hair, she led him to one of the empty chairs.

Adjusting his position, Adam said, "Bobby was certainly in rare form last night. He seemed to enjoy the couple of shots we had together."

"I think he had a couple even before we got there," Mel said. "That's not unusual for those guys, especially when Sunny's not around."

"They do seem to indulge a good bit," Adam noted.

"One of the side effects of working behind a bar," Mel said. "Some people can handle it. Some can't. The fallout from drinking is a big part of the business." She sprayed water on his hair. "You don't see too many old bartenders," she added.

Adam said nothing for a moment, enjoying the gentle spray. "Has Bobby worked at Smitty's a long time?" he asked.

"He's been there about five years," Mel answered. "He was an O.C. cop before that. He worked part-time at the Clarion during that time, and then..." She hesitated. "Things changed, so he decided to leave the police force and he ended up at Smitty's." Adam hesitated himself before commenting. "Things do change in life, don't they?"

"That they do," she acknowledged. She combed her fingers through his hair. "How do you want it?"

"Short... real short... like I used to wear it."

Mel made no comment. The hair cut continued a few minutes and then she said, "Bobby's like you in a lot of ways."

"How so?"

"He's very protective of his private life."

Adam couldn't help but laugh. The clicking of the scissors stopped. "Did I say something funny?" Mel asked.

"No," Adam quickly responded. "It's just that when I went into the bar the first time, I wasn't there several minutes before Bobby started quizzing me about my life–my story, as he later called it."

"He is good at that," Mel acknowledged.

Without thinking, Adam spurted out, "he even looked me up on the Internet." "Yeah, he told me you're a brain surgeon," Mel said. "But I already knew that."

"How did you know that?" Adam challenged, unable to hide the surprise from his voice.

"You said it yourself–the day you and Bobby made the bet for a bottle of B&B. I had you figured for not being a betting man; and if you were, it would only be on a sure thing."

"Why didn't you say something?" Adam asked curiously.

Mel shrugged her shoulders. "I figured when you wanted me to know, you'd tell me."

"One of the side effects of success is the fame that comes with it, and that isn't always a positive thing," Adam said softly.

"I would think the positives outweigh the negatives," Mel commented.

"You would think..." He let the sentence trail off. "Anyway, Bobby's an interesting work of art."

"He says the same thing about you, only with different words."

Adam wanted to ask just what the bartender said, but chose not to go there. He didn't want to unlatch Pandora's Box.

The haircut complete, Mel brushed off the back of Adam's neck with a powder-filled barber brush. She said, "Don't be too critical of Bobby. He tries to learn something about all his customers, and if he took the time to look you up on the Internet, that means he likes you. You've made an impression on him, and not many people have."

Deciding enough had been said, Adam paid the bill and prepared to leave. As he did, he noticed the old lady under the hair dryer. "You'd better go tend to that lady over there. Looks like she's sound asleep."

Mel looked over her shoulder and chuckled. "She sleeps there all the time. Claims it's the best sleep she gets all week."

Adam hesitated. "You gonna be there tonight?"

Mel looked back at him and tipped her head to the side. While they had met there on numerous occasions over the past months, it was the first time the rendezvous was preplanned. "Maybe."

"Maybe?"

Her smile widened. "I'll maybe be there around nine. How's that sound."

"Nice."

Mel laughed and shook her head.

"What's so funny?" Adam demanded in a friendly voice.

"You two are really a pair." With that, she turned and headed toward Sleeping Beauty in the back.

"You two are a pain," Mel mouthed softly as the door closed and Adam disappeared from view. "What are you and I?" She forced a chuckle as a way of hiding her nervousness from the question. She knew what she wanted, which was to take it to the next step–whatever that might be. The question, however, what did Adam want? That was still very much a mystery. He said little about himself, much less his feelings. For the most part, he remained withdrawn–continuing to struggle with whatever caused him to close his shell. She didn't know, but guessed it was a personal tragedy of immense proportions. She just wished he'd let her in, if only a little. She could help, she was sure. After all...

She cut the thought off as Sleeping Beauty woke from her nap.

Third Wednesday in August

Adam took the first empty seat available. Sliding the stool closer, he leaned forward and looked around. It was still busy with the left over lunch crowd combined with a few golf foursomes after a morning on the links. Doug was at the far end mixing some sort of concoction, and Sunny was just coming out of the kitchen with a basket of wings. She saw Adam and held up a finger indicating she'd be with him in a minute. Adam smiled and waved her off, indicating he was in no hurry. He looked around again. It was Wednesday afternoon and there was no Bobby.

As promised, Sunny was there a short time later with his drink. "How you doing today, Adam?"

"I'm okay," Adam said. "Don't usually see you behind the bar this time of day," Adam said.

Sunny nodded in agreement. "Bobby had to take a couple hours off."

"Sick?"

"No, something to do with the kids."

"Oh," Adam said, struggling to hide his surprise. Bobby never said anything about having children.

Sunny continued. "He should be here soon." She pointed over her shoulder. "He just lives around the corner."

"Oh yeah, where?"

"Last house on the left."

"He can walk to work, huh?"

Sunny laughed. "He often comes in running. They're great kids, but boy do they give him a run for his money... no pun intended."

Adam smiled and took a sip of his drink.

"Anyway, let me know if you want something to eat," Sunny said. "Bertha made shrimp salad earlier, and it's pretty good. Shrimp are nice and fresh."

The suggestion stimulated his gastric juices. "Okay, how about on rye toast?"

"Lettuce and tomato?"

"Sure."

"Fries?"

Adam laughed as he wondered who taught whom the art of running up a bar tab? "Sure," he repeated.

As Adam returned to his drink, a side of his brain told him that what he just heard was none of his business. Mel even said that Bobby kept his personal life close to his vest. Which was fine, Adam guessed, but Bobby didn't play the *what goes around comes around* game fairly. Hell, the bartender looked Adam up on the Internet. Wasn't turnabout fair play?

Sunny brought out the shrimp salad, which was as good as promised. His drink was refreshed and Adam focused on subduing his hunger pains. During this time, he talked to a couple of newbies as well as a couple of barfriends. As usual, conversations were kept superficial and light. Talk was cheap so long as it wasn't deep.

He left a short time later and started across the parking lot towards home. At the last moment, however, he turned and headed down the road behind the bar. It ran along the water; and like most waterfront communities, there was a wide mixture of houses. The gamut ran from relatively new two story mansions to single story shacks that looked as if they'd blow over in the next nor'easter. There was the usual mixture of empty trailers, boats and other *crapola* cluttering up the driveways, yet the yards themselves were neat and tidy.

Adam walked at a leisurely pace. He was in no particular hurry, still unsure of what he was doing and why. Which was bogus, of course. He knew exactly what he was doing. He was a very curious person. If there was a question... a mystery... a challenge... he tackled it. If someone said something couldn't be done, he'd find a way to do it. While he could never claim a hundred percent success in his profession, some of his outcomes were staggering. He thought back to the beginning of it all. It was his first year of surgical residency at Hopkins when some big-wig from another university (he couldn't even remember the man's name) gave a lecture on conjoined twins. He said there was a growing demand for the service world-wide as global communication brought these cases more and more to the forefront. Unfortunately, the intricacies and surgical technique were years away from even beginning to think about separating these unfortunate patients, especially those connected at the head. The man rambled on for the customary sixty minutes, showing slides from his travels all over the world. It was the most interesting lecture Adam had ever attended.

Three months later, Adam was accepted into the pediatric neurosurgery residency program at

Johns Hopkins. Now, whenever asked about his progression into the field, he always answered with a laugh, "My career was launched by a man whose name I don't even remember."

He walked another five minutes before coming to the end. The road dissected a peninsula that jutted into Assawoman Bay. The house to the right was newly built and vacant. There was a for sale sign in the front yard and a box with fliers. A large trash dumpster overflowing with construction debris sat off to the side. It looked like the house was ready for occupancy. All it needed was some grass in the front yard... and a buyer. Adam reached into the box and pulled out a flyer. He guessed a million and was short by fifty percent. He shook his head side to side. Maybe he was in the wrong business, he thought. He walked across the dirt yard. He stopped beside the dumpster and turned around.

The house across the street–the last house on the left–was an older two story Cape Cod. It sat on the largest lot on the block, and had water in the back and on the far side. The house looked in excellent condition, although the fenced-in yard had toys strewn about. There was a large covered front porch with an old fashioned swing. It looked like a typical house for a typical family.

Starting to feel guilty, Adam turned to head back up the road when there was a sudden commotion from the house. The front door flew open and three children–two boys and a girl–came running out onto the porch. The girl was the oldest. Adam guessed about twelve or thirteen. The boys were a couple of years younger. All three were laughing and yelling as they tore down the steps. A moment later, Bobby came running around the corner, a large golden retriever at his heels. The kids headed towards the front gate, but Bobby was too fast. He caught two of the three by the arms. There was more laughter and then the front door opened again. Mel stepped out onto the porch. "You guys had better be quiet. You're going to wake up the whole neighborhood."

"They're already awake," one of the children yelled back. The dog barked to add its two cents to the ordeal.

During all this, Adam hid behind the dumpster. He brought his hand up to his chest in an effort to slow his racing heart. He pressed up against the metal and closed his eyes. He could no longer see, but he could still hear.

"When are you going to be home?" one of the boys said.

"Way past your bedtime," Bobby answered.

"Can we wait up for you?"

"You know it's a school night," Bobby scolded.

"It's summer!"

Mel's voice boomed from the porch. "You kids had better get in here and eat your lunch, or I'm going to feed it to the dog."

Good-byes were shouted and the children could be heard stampeding back up to the porch. Bobby yelled that they had better all listen to Mel, or else.

Adam heard the front door slam shot, the front gate open and then rapid footsteps as Bobby headed up the street. It was a good fifteen minutes before Adam moved out from behind the dumpster.

By then, his level of curiosity had risen beyond his level of guilt.

8

Mid-September 2008

It didn't take long to learn, listening to the conversations around him, that deer season had opened that morning. Adam tried remembering if he heard any gunshots during the day, but recalled none. When Bobby brought him his first drink, Adam mentioned this to the bartender who replied, "Bow season started today. Muzzleloaders are a couple weeks away."

"Oh," Adam said. "You bow hunt?"

The guy sitting next to Adam–one of the semi-regulars–spoke up. "Bobby here's the best bow shooter on the eastern shore. Why it was about this time last year Bobby got himself a five hundred pound mule. Ain't that right Bobby? Go on, tell him about the time you shot the farmer's mule. Dropped him dead in his tracks, too." The man laughed loudly.

"Shut the fuck up," Bobby demanded, a thin smile across his face.

Adam smiled as well. A couple months before, he would have kept his mouth shut. Now, however..."I've never had mule before. What's it taste like?"

"You shut up, too," Bobby directed.

The guy sitting next to Adam said, "I can still see it plain as day. It was a beautiful morning. The sky was dead clear. No breeze... Sun was starting to break over the tree tops. We had just finished breakfast with the farmer whose land we hunted and were heading out to our tree stands. All of a sudden, this huge buck comes bounding out of the woods into the pasture right in front of us. Well, if you know Bobby, there isn't much that causes him to hesitate. In one fell swoop, he snatched an arrow from his quiver, loaded up, took aim and let her fly. It was a perfect shot, too, except for one thing. Just as the arrow was about to strike its mark, the ole buck leaped high in the air. The arrow passed right under his belly. No harm done, except for another thing. Right behind the deer was the farmer's mule, just munching on some grass, oblivious to everything." A sip of beer was had, "Well, the arrow struck the mule right in the heart. The animal took one step and dropped right in its tracks. A perfect shot."

"What happened next?" Adam said, trying to contain his own laughter.

"Why, the old farmer, he was mad as hell. He looked at Bobby and said as he started shaking in his boots. 'You shot my mule, boy. You shot ole

Hercules.' Needless to say, Bobby here had to turn a lot of tips to pay for that fine trophy. We ain't been back to that farm since. It was good huntin' there, too."

"So did you guys go hunting this morning?" Adam asked, still laughing.

"That we did," the guy said. "But we didn't see shit. Three days before when we were scouting the area, there were deer all over the fuckin' place. Today though, nothing."

Adam smiled. "Sounds like the deer down here are smart."

"A lot smarter than most people give 'em credit for."

Just then, Sunny strolled by. "How about you, Sunny," Adam said. "Do you hunt?"

Sunny stopped and smiled. "Bobby was going to take me out one day last year, but when he came down with a bad case of chiggers, I decided hunting and me probably wouldn't do too well together."

The guy next to Adam piped in. "Sunny's idea of hunting is to ride through the San Diego Zoo in her Hummer with an Uzi hanging out the window. Can't you see her in a pink designer camouflage suit?"

"You only wished you looked so good in camouflage," Sunny spouted.

Smiles were exchanged and the evening wore on with Adam continuing to wonder about the taste of mule.

End of October 2008

Needless to say, Halloween was an experience at Smitty McGee's. People of all ages, shapes and sizes donned costumes and piled in as early as mid-afternoon. Adam was forewarned of the spectacle. He didn't dress up, of course. Mel did. She closed her shop early and made a grand entrance as a lady vampire. Adam couldn't claim to have met many vampires in his life. He did suspect Mel was one of the better looking ones–at least to him, she was.

It was a festive occasion. The entire bar was transformed into a haunted house with decorations everywhere. Even the windows had been painted into colorful scenes. *Beach House* was playing, the music loud, Ricky sang in tune and the dance floor was full. People seemed to be having a good time. Even Adam was in good spirits. Mel led him through the crowd, introducing him to various people–some were new, some he had met before. Besides, Sunny appointed Mel as one of the judges for the best costume contest, and the hairdresser-now-Halloween-judge wanted to make sure she got a look at everyone.

Movement was slow and tedious. Not only did you have to worry about spilling your drink, you had to avoid being probed and prodded by a piece of someone's costume. After a while, Adam decided the prodding and probing couldn't be avoided. He then directed all his energy to not spilling his drink... and keeping up with Mel, who seemed to be having a much easier time navigating through the crowd.

Time passed quickly, and before Adam realized it, it was 11 o'clock–the appointed hour for the prizes to be handed out. He stood in the background as the winners were announced. Coming over to refill his drink, Bobby asked, "What do you think of all this, Doc?"

"Well, Bobby, there's just nothing like being in the men's room, standing next to a guy wearing wings on his back."

Yes, Halloween was an experience at Smitty McGee's, or any bar in the area for that matter.

*****

Other times were an experience as well. Such as the night Adam watched a young couple dancing. Unfamiliar with the modern day dance steps, Adam leaned over to Mel and said, "What's the name of that dance?"

Mel laughed. "I don't think it has a name."

Bobby, who happened to be standing nearby replied, "That ain't dancing. That's just plain stump grinding."

Adam and Mel looked at one another. Mel laughed. Adam blushed.

*****

She was tall. She was blonde. She was thin. She was built. She was plain downright beautiful. Adam said to Bobby, who was also eying up the newly arrived customer, "Who is that?"

"Don't know her name," Bobby said without breaking off his glance. "She comes in once in a while, usually alone, sometimes with a couple of girlfriends. She drinks wine only, and eats a lot of salads. We just call her Daddy Long Legs."

And so she was.

*****

Adam had been watching the staff that roamed back and forth behind the bar. Besides the normal bartenders (if bartenders could be called normal!) there were the bar backs, food runners and even an occasional waitress who lost her way. The space was narrow, and while the comings and goings of the various people looked chaotic, in reality, it was a well-choreographed ballet. Sometimes two people passed with simply a "Behind ya!" Sometimes they passed in silence–

almost as if they possessed radar. What they did have was a good understanding of what it took to work behind the bar, and to do so efficiently. Mastering the ballet was one of the first requirements for any new employee.

On this particular night, there was an additional component to the choreography Adam had not noticed before. There was a certain amount of flirtation that went on between the staff–a gentle bump here, a touch there. There was even the occasional whisper or quiet comment that often resulted in a smile, a comeback comment, or maybe even a blush–although Adam suspected it took a lot for people in the beverage business to exhibit the latter. There was never anything totally inappropriate, but said actions were close to the edge at times.

Adam turned up his people watching skills as the choreography became even more interesting. He saw Bobby behind Sunny with one hand full of beer, the other hand free to rub gently across her back. Adam was sure there was more to the motion than simply letting the bar owner know there was someone behind her. The action was repeated on Bobby's return trip. Sunny, who was in an active conversation with an older couple sitting across from her, didn't bat an eye. She shrugged her shoulders slightly as if feeling an electrical charge up her spine.

Adam took a sip of his drink and slowly

scanned the bar. In one sweep of the head, he saw three similar behaviors, including a boob rub against the back of Bobby as one of the young food runners passed by. Taking another sip, Adam wondered how anyone could concentrate back there with all the shenanigans going on. The ballet continued to the music of the Bourbon Tabernacle Choir.

He enjoyed watching this newly discovered behavior until it was cut short by Bobby, who came by with a refill of V.O. Shoving the bottle back into the ice tray, the bartender said, "You seem to be a lot more intense tonight than normal."

Adam blushed. (He was obviously not bar server material.) "Things go on behind the bar a lot of people don't even realize," he said.

Bobby leaned forward and flashed one of his infamous toothpaste commercial smiles. "Things go on behind the bar that you don't see. Like human nature everywhere, bar people are always on the prowl. But unlike other species of the human race, people in the bar business never seem to find what they are looking for–and if they do, it's short lived."

"Why's that?" Adam inquired.

"Simple," Bobby replied. "No one in the bar business is loyal. The F.U.R. of any relationship here probably approaches 90%, maybe even higher."

"F.U.R.?" Adam said.

Bobby smiled. "Yeah, the fuck up rate." Another smile and the bartender was gone. He didn't take three steps, however, before his hand touched the bottom of the young food runner who had boob caressed him a few minutes before. Bobby looked Adam's way and gave him a wink.

Adam shook his head and smiled.

*****

Bobby nodded toward the band (Beach House) where Sparks, the harmonica player was taking the lead and adding a significant amount of love hormones to the air. "Sparks claims he doesn't know how to read music. Says he plays everything by ear," Bobby said.

A middle aged man with long blond hair a couple seats down from Adam said, "then why does he need so many God damn harmonicas? He only has two ears."

Bobby laughed. "I think he's full of shit anyway. He plays too well not to be able to read music."

"I agree," the man said.

The others nodded. Adam scanned the crowd that had toned down a few decibels once Sparks started playing. No matter what the age of the couple in question, the sound of the harmonica filled the air with a sense of romance. Bobby called it foreplay. Adam thought it was something more than that, but didn't argue the point. He took a deep breath and turned toward the nearest TV screen. ESPN was on with no volume. He watched anyway. His vision blurred, his mind focusing on topics other than sports. He listened to the music as the noise in the room continued to soften. He felt warm. His arms started to tingle. His forehead broke out in a sweat. He could feel his heartbeat in his ear. He shook his head side to side to clear the sensations. Then he stopped. He didn't want the feeling to subside. It felt good. It had been a long time since...

He turned back toward the band. The sound of the harmonica filled the air. Sparks and the band played on.

Adam watched... and waited... and hoped Mel would arrive soon.

*****

The third B&B of the night was served, tapped on the bar and downed quickly. Sunny was on the prowl. Chasing the liquor with a mouthful of V.O., Adam said, "I've been meaning to ask you, have I ever paid you for any of these shots?"

Bobby tipped his head to the side, the normal smile fading. "Why are you asking a dumb ass question like that?"

Adam tipped his own head to the side and flashed his barfriend the bird.

The smile returned on the bartender's face. "You know Doc, there's hope for you yet."

*****

Adam sat in his recliner staring out the patio door, across the empty lots, past the tree line and out across Dirickson's Creek. He wondered about Mr. Dirickson... or was it Mrs. Dirickson the creek was named after? Who were they? What did they look like? What was his or her story? Did they have tragedy in their lives? Adam figured they probably did. Everyone does, he thought.

He rolled his neck to work out a kink. He heard a snap and the pain eased. He told himself he should get up and do something... something besides sit in the recliner all day. Day in and day out, hours on end, he sat staring across the empty lots. "Symbolic," he muttered. He told himself it was time to...

"Time to do what?" he mouthed angrily. Bobby said there was hope for him yet. Aloud, "But hope for what?" Then he chuckled. "You know the answer."

The sound of Sparks playing the harmonica flowed forth. He thought of the feeling that encompassed him sitting at the bar. It subsided, only to return a short time later when Mel walked through the door. Was there hope for him... for her... for them?

The stare continued, focused at first before gradually becoming a blur. Darkness followed as he drifted off to sleep.

*****

A nomination for the world's weirdest liquor: bacon flavored vodka.

9

November 2008

It was the Thursday before Thanksgiving. The crowd was sparse and especially quiet. Half the TVs were already off. The green drape was down, indicating the back section was closed. Beach House was playing a song Ricky had written in his Nashville days. It was a ballad about the Chesapeake Bay and had become one of Adam's favorites. Besides pleasant to listen to, it always had a calming effect on the crowd. The song ended to scattered applause. Eye contact was made, heads nodded and thank you's mouthed. While the band enjoyed themselves whenever they played, they were especially fond of Thursday nights.

Adam felt the same way. He hadn't missed a Thursday night in over a month. Neither had Mel, who was sitting at his side. As usual, their conversation was friendly and upbeat. They talked about a lot of things. They talked about a lot of nothing. Both seemed to accept their relationship for what it was... drinking buddies at a bar. Barfriends.

Adam imagined that in reality Mel was looking for more than a barfriend. He imagined a lot of things, but was quick to cut those thoughts off. He maintained his discipline—out of the cave, but not too far. An occasional warm and tingling feeling was enough. He needed nothing more. He wanted nothing more.

He kept telling himself that.

Following a country western song, Ricky announced it was time for a short break. As the others mingled with the crowd on the dance floor, Ricky grabbed his beer and headed their way. "Evening, folks, how's it going tonight?" he asked.

"Fine, thanks." Adam said.

"Hey, guy," Mel said. She leaned forward and gave the band leader a kiss on the cheek.

Ricky focused his attention on Adam. "I've seen you around lately. Thanks for coming out."

"My pleasure," Adam said.

"If there's anything you want to hear, let us know," Ricky said. "If we can do it, fine. If not, we'll fake it somehow."

Adam smiled.

"Believe me, they do a lot of that," Mel injected.

Ricky laughed. "Anything to please the crowd." He took a sip of his beer. "Speaking of which, Mel, several people have asked if you're going to join us for a song or two."

Mel blushed as she glanced over at Adam, whose eyes had widened.

"She has a beautiful voice," Ricky directed to Adam. "You ought to hear her."

"It's been a while," Mel said.

"Like riding a bike," Ricky quipped. He nodded before moving on to talk with other patrons.

Recovering from his surprise, Adam said, "You never told me you could sing."

Mel looked away and sipped her wine. "There're a lot of things we haven't told one another...but that's okay."

There was so much she wanted to tell him... about herself... about her life.

None of it was bad. She wasn't a serial killer, a secret FBI agent or anything exciting like that. Her life was plain and simple, her days routine and predictable, her future cloudy as the unpredictability of the economy was washing over all the businesses in the area.

Hers was no exception. Yet, while it was a struggle, she was surviving... physically at least.

She gave Adam a soft kiss on the cheek as she slid off the bar stool. "I'm going to hit the ladies room. I'll be back."

Adam watched as she made her way around the bar. She was slow in her walk, speaking to several people on the way. At the head of the bar, she stopped and chatted with the crowd that had gathered around the band. There were a lot of smiles and a few laughs. She seemed to know everyone, and everyone seemed to know her.

"Why not?" Adam thought. She was a local.

He broke off his watch and focused on his glass of V.O. Mel was right, there were a lot of things they didn't know about each other. It was the way he wanted it. It was the way it had to be. Still, it would be nice to get to know her more. What other secrets did she hide? But he knew to learn those secrets; he'd have to let out a few of his own.

He swirled the ice around and took a sip. He waited for the aftertaste to pass before taking another. Setting the glass down, his hand subconsciously went up to his cheek. One spot in particular felt soft and moist. It was as if her lips were still there. It was like...

His thoughts were interrupted by the sound of music restarting. As he spun around, he registered another look of surprise. Mel was standing at the mike. She waited patiently as a round of applause subsided. "We have a request for a Beatles' song. It's been a while, but we'll give it a go." She turned and nodded to Ricky.

The beginning of *Yesterday* came forth. He had heard the melody numerous times, but never paid much attention to the lyrics.

That is until now.

As Ricky promised, Mel's voice was beautiful. "Yesterday, all my troubles seemed so far away..."

The song continued. Mel sang it beautifully. Adam listened intensely, mesmerized by her voice. It was like church bells ringing in his head. His blood warmed. His spine tingled. His toes even curled up in his shoes. He felt good... perhaps even more than good.

The song ended. Mel blushed at the intensity of the applause from such a small crowd. She succumbed to the demand for another. When finished, she made her way back to her seat. A fresh glass of wine was waiting. Adam was not. She motioned to Bobby who came over. The expression on her face asked the obvious question.

"He said he had to step outside a few minutes," Bobby said. "If I didn't know better, I'd say he had tears in his eyes."

"Thanks," Mel said. She grabbed her glass and Adam's drink, and slid off the stool.

She found him in the back leaning up against one of the bulkhead pilings. He was staring out across the water. The sky was clear, the moon nearly full. Lights from Ocean City flickered in the distance. A gentle crisp breeze blew in their faces, otherwise it was quiet. She walked up to him and held out his glass. He took it without comment. "Beautiful night," she said softly.

"That it is," he said. He took a sip of his drink. "So was your voice."

"Thank you. I'm glad you liked it," she said. There was so much more Mel wanted to say, so much she wanted to do. Yet she knew that *silence was golden* fit well tonight. She told herself she'd know when it was time for the next step, whatever that might be. For now, she told herself to be content just being at his side.

Time passed. Seconds? Minutes?

Days... months... years... How long had it been?

How long had it been since she felt this way about anyone? How long had it been since she'd been this close to anyone.

Close, yet so far. She knew he was in pain. She wanted to take him in her arms and whisper in his ear and say that she understood. She understood because she too was in pain. If he would only let her in, she could help.

Days... months... years... It had been a long time since anyone had let her into their lives. The reverse was also true.

Silence remained golden. Then unexpectedly, Adam turned to her. He looked deep into her eyes... deep and in a way she had not experienced before. A chill went up her spine as he said, "I want to tell you just how lovely you were tonight. You have a beautiful voice. You're a beautiful person, too. I didn't fully realize either until tonight." She started to speak, but a finger went across her lips. He continued. "I know we don't know each other very well. I know we each have our own secrets... not necessarily anything bad, just secrets. Like Bobby says, everybody has a story. And I can't expect you to share yours until I'm ready to do the same."

Mel reached up and removed his finger from her lips. She resisted the urge to caress it with her tongue. "You may think I can't understand, but I do. At least partially, I do." To her surprise, he leaned in and gently kissed her on the lips. It was their first real kiss. It was a soft gentle kiss. It was lovely. Time stood still a moment, and then he broke away. From the reflection of the moon, she watched as tears rolled down his cheeks. He said nothing. She remained silent as well.

The next step had just been taken.

*****

The following night, Ricky was there with the whole band. The crowd was its usual self–loud, rowdy and having a good time. Mel and Adam sat near the bend, lucky to find seats together. Mel was playing Buzztime and Adam was watching the ballet behind the bar. Because it was crowded, they were forced to sit close to one another, something they had been doing more and more of late, even when there was room on either side. It wasn't a strange sensation, just new... not unpleasant, but new.

The band started playing again and Adam turned to watch. He noticed Angie was standing at a mike. She was Alex the drummer's wife, and came in with him most nights. She occasionally sang a few duets with Ricky or a solo or two. She had a low gravely blues voice, one that tended to sooth your soul, as Bobby liked to call it. For Adam, her voice was captivating.

Things were no different tonight as she sang: "Oh, baby, what you do to me..."

Adam looked over at Mel, who was locked in a tight trivia match with several other players. He smiled and let his leg rub up against hers. She responded with pressure of her own, but that was all. Her stare and facial expression remained the same. That was fine with Adam as his thoughts returned to the night before. They were outside by the water, looking up at the moon. They kissed. It was a wonderful kiss... so sweet... so soft... so...

His eyes refocused on Mel.

"Oh, baby, what you do to me..."

10

December 2008

It was a quiet Thursday evening at Smitty's. The crowd was sparse as winter engulfed the area. The night before, the temperature dropped below freezing. Every time the door opened, the cold burst through, reminding customers what await-ed them when they left. Adam suspected it would be a late leaving crowd tonight.

Through it all, Ricky and Sal played on. They were oblivious to the thinness of the crowd, to the noise around them (yes, it was still noisy), to the televisions flashing their usual array of visual stimulation, to the changing weather outside. Ricky and Sal were musicians, and that's what they did.

The particular song at the moment was a gentle country piece. The lyrics told the story of a young boy leaving home for the first time to go off to work. As the song continued, Adam noticed a tall distinguished older man sitting alone at the far corner. He was sipping beer from a bottle as he too watched intently. Whether intentional or not, he caught Ricky's eye. Nods and smiles were exchanged. Ricky had the knack of catching the eyes of various patrons while he was playing, making them feel special, connecting them to the band in a unique way. Bobby called it business flirting. Adam had little doubt it was the personality of the musicians as well as their music that kept the same people coming back week after week.

Anyway, the man in question took another sip of beer before rising to his feet. He wandered over to the band stand, nodded again to Ricky and Sal, picked up the base guitar sitting in its rack, threw the strap over his head and started playing. He picked the song up without hesitation and without missing a note.

It was a subtle addition to the sound mix, but even Adam's naive ear could tell the difference. The man was good. He made the duo a trio the next several songs. When he was finished, he acknowledged the applause, put the guitar back in its place and went back to his designated stool where a fresh bottle awaited him.

When Bobby passed by, Adam asked the obvious question, "Who was that masked rider?"

Bobby answered in his normal gentle Oxford educated manner. "Fuck if I know. Never saw the man before."

Just then, the door opened and a burst of cold air poured in.

*****

The night led to an even colder Sunday afternoon. There was an inch of snow on the ground. The football season was half over. The much antici- pated Cowboys-Redskins rivalry was on many of the screens around the bar. The game was tied with neither team showing signs of greatness. The bar was crowded, the noise level a little subdued at the moment. It was halftime. Several seats down from Adam sat two elderly men–one wear- ing a Cowboys' jersey, the other a Redskins' jersey. They were arguing vehemently over which team had the better half. As they were drunk, their voices were loud and getting unruly. A fight was surely about to erupt. Coming out of the kitchen with a food order, Bobby first heard and then saw the action. He sat the food down in front of the appropriate customers and then swag- gered–at a quick pace–down to where the two football fans were sitting. He grabbed a bottle of Jack Daniels on the way. Noticing that Bobby was moving at a much faster pace, much of the crowd turned to see where he was headed. A fast moving Bobby meant there was action about to break out somewhere down the bar.

The two old men didn't see him at first, but did stop arguing as he refilled their glasses with the sour mash beverage. As they each reached for their respective bar crystal, Bobby's hands dropped across the tops. He leaned forward and said in a very loud voice, "If you two don't settle down, I'm going to first cut you off, and then I'm going to call the authorities."

"The authorities?" the Cowboys fan said.

"Yeah, the authorities... the AARP."

"You mean that old folks organization?"

"That's the one," Bobby acknowledged.

"What the hell they going to do?" the Redskins fan challenged.

"Come in here and take your asses directly to a nursing home. I understand they have a couple openings in eastern Pennsylvania... right next door to the Eagles' training camp."

The two men looked at one another, and then back at Bobby. "Before or after the game is over?" the Cowboys fan asked.

Bobby gave them one of his patented smiles. Taking his hands off the glasses, he pushed them forward. "Cheers."

The two men broke into smiles. "Cheers."

As Bobby walked away, one of the men said, "Right next to the Eagles training camp!"

"Why, that would be downright torture," said the other.

With that, everyone's attention returned to the TV screens. Halftime was over.

The following Friday

Adam had been around long enough to have heard most of Ricky and the band's repertoire. It was impressively vast. There were many favorites, some requested on a regular basis, some just played, but the song that amazed Adam the most was *Teenage Wasted*. While Adam didn't quite get the gist of the song's appeal, it did fill the dancing space in front of the band no matter what mix the crowd on any given night.

On this particular night, an elderly lady, all dolled up as if she were still a teenager herself, was out in the middle of the pack. She was dancing with no one in particular, and no one seemed to mind her presence. She smiled at everyone and they smiled back. That wouldn't have been so bad, except for one small detail... She couldn't dance.

Bobby happened to buzz by just as the event was happening. He paused a moment and watched. "You know, Adam, I haven't seen hips move like that since someone had a seizure in here a couple years back."

"That's what they call it–the epileptic seizure dance," Adam said.

Bobby laughed. "You know, Adam, I've said it before, there's hope for you yet."

Then he was gone. The song continued. Unfortunately, so did the dance.

*****

One thing you could never complain about at Smitty's was the lack of auditory and visual stimulation. What was playing on any TV screen at any time was generally left up to the people near-by. The only exception was that one of the screens near Bobby's station was always tuned to the Outdoor Channel. Bobby's explanation, "If the sport doesn't involve something I can't eat at the end, then I'm not interested. Besides, a bartender should keep his eyes on the customers, not on the game. Bobby took a quick look around, and then focused back on Adam. "When you're in the operating room, aren't there usually a lot of distractions going on?"

Adam laughed at the comparison. "Sure."

"Didn't it take you time to learn how to adjust to all that... knowing which sounds were important and which weren't?"

"Yes, it does take getting used to."

"Maybe all your young doctors-in-training ought to come here and bartend for a week or so before they go into the operating room."

Adam laughed again.

Bobby stared him down without joining in the joviality of the moment. "I'm serious," he said.

"Think about it."

Adam spun around on his chair and focused on the sounds and sights around him. At the same time, he focused on what was not there. There was no beeping of a respirator signaling the patient's heart was still beating. There were no swishing bellows as air was systematically pumped into a set of lungs. He could not hear the air handling system as it filtered the air, capturing any bacteria that dared trespass into the sterile environment. There was no clanging of heavy metal instruments being made ready for his command. There was no snapping of needle holders around delicate yet sharp suturing needles. The phone that always seemed to ring at the most inopportune times could not be heard. There were no soft conversations in the corner between the nurse and whoever she might be chatting with at the time. Finally, there was no surgical resident showing off to the younger medical student who might be scrubbed, pointing out in grave detail every piece of anatomy and or every particular act the attending surgeon might be performing at the moment.

Instead, there was the crowd at the bar, some standing, some sitting. Their muted conversations added to the decibel level and the atmosphere. There was constant noise behind the bar as the three bartenders plus the supporting cast performed their ballet. The band continued playing, oblivious to the goings on around them. A few people were in front of the band dancing, one middle age woman was flirting with Ricky as she bounced her oversized body about. Surrounding it all were the voiceless television screens spewing out a variety of visual entertainment.

The atmosphere was certainly not the same as an operating room, yet, as Bobby suggested, lessons about concentration could be learned. Adam spun around and faced the bar. He emptied his glass and pushed it forward for a refill. He wondered what other lessons might be learned.

*****

For whatever reason, people often wanted to get up and play with Rickie and the band. Sometimes the results weren't bad, like the night the man played the base, or when Mel and Angie sang. There was another gentleman who occasionally sat at the drums. Some of the regular ladies played along with a tambourine or other percussion instruments. Then there was this middle aged blond who always wanted to sing a song or two. She was pretty to look at. She was a regular who usually brought a group of friends with her. Her boyfriend a decade older than her, was quick with the refills and often pulled out the shot monkey–shots all around. So as one might expect, she got her chance.

Only she couldn't sing. The first time he heard her, Adam suffered through the few minutes of torture. The next, he did make a comment, asking Bobby when they started offering karaoke.

Bobby answered with one of his smiles. "She thinks she's the Fenwick Idol."

*****

Adam watched the middle aged couple sitting across the bar, or rather she was sitting and he was standing at her side. He wore a long sleeved shirt with a Harley Davidson design on the back and clean but ragged looking jeans. She was decked out in a matching shirt, only one that fit much tighter. Her jeans were much newer. His hair, unkempt, was stuffed beneath a non-descript hat with dirt on the brim. Her hair, freshly washed for the occasion, was pulled in a ponytail and hung well below her shoulder line.

She leaned back and extended her neck. He bent his head down toward her. Their lips met. Their kiss was long and passionate. It was not the first such action of the evening. Nor did Adam suspect it would be the last. He watched a moment before turning away, thinking–two different people... one couple. He wondered about their stories... individually and as a couple? But regardless of the answers, he knew their actions here were just the beginning of their evening... and continuation of their future. Some would call it foreplay. Adam, however, realized it went far deeper than that. Today's gentle caress could be felt a lifetime.

Mel's leg up against his interrupted Adam's thoughts. He looked her way. She looked at him, smiled and returned to her game. Adam turned away, thinking: two different people, one...

For the first time in many months, he thought about his own future.

Middle of December

Sunny was walking up and down the bar late one evening and noticed the atmosphere had become exceptionally subdued. The regulars were there, talking in the corner as they do. A couple of semi-regulars were scattered about and a couple newbies were looking over menus. Adam sat sipping his drink and watching Mel play Buzztime. Sunny passed by Bobby with a concerned look on her face and announced in a rather loud voice, "We need shots."

After the round of complimentary shots, the place did get louder, drink orders were refilled and Sunny looked much happier.

A short time later, Adam finished his own shot,

looked at his watch and then at the near empty glass of whisky. Last call was fast approaching. He told himself he should get up and get going. He had stayed much longer than planned, and even though it was cold, it was a beautiful night for a walk. Only his body wasn't listening. It was content to stay put. He sucked in a deep breath and told himself to be careful. His frequency and length of stays were increasing, especially when Mel was at his side. He knew, however, it was more than that. And it was more than just people watching. He came here because of the want, the desire to be with other people. "Camaraderie," he mouthed. He felt safe here–out of his cave, but with the entrance nearby. "Camaraderie with caution," he added.

Just a few months ago, he was basically house bound, unable to break out of the self-imposed bubble. During the first few weeks, it was a struggle to even go to the store. Phone calls and emails went unanswered. The only person he communicated with was Carol, his administrative assistant, and those emails were brief and to the point. Yes, he was okay. No, he didn't need anything. Yes, she should continue handling his personal affairs. Lately, however, he found himself venturing further from the cave. There was a sense of pleasure sitting at the bar, having a drink, looking around, listening to the music, watching the soundless television, watching the

113

ballet behind the bar. He was even beginning to talk to other people–barfriends, as they were called. He was careful what he said, but he was conversing nonetheless.

He glanced up and down the bar. The only people left were faces he recognized. "I'm becoming a regular like them," he thought with a frown. As an afterthought, he decided that was okay. Out of the cave, but close to the entrance. He emptied his glass and slid it forward. Having already paid his tab, he slid off the stool, bid Mel goodnight, insisted he wanted to walk home and headed for the door. He fought the urge to look back for a final glance. As he stepped into the night, he took in a deep breath and headed across the parking lot.

Yes, it was a beautiful night for a walk.

11

The week before Christmas

"Here's one for the book," Bobby said, refilling Adam's glass.

"What book?" Adam interrupted.

"The book you and I are going to write."

Adam could only laugh.

Bobby continued. "Anyway, this happened maybe two or three stools to your left there. A young bartender that used to work here went up to a regular one night who was here with a couple buddies, and said 'I'm going to ask you for your daughter's telephone number, and I strongly suspect you're going to give it to me.' Before the customer could protest, the bartender showed the man a picture on his cell phone from the week before... and it wasn't one of his buddies sitting next to him either." Bobby paused and gave Adam a big smile. "You know, that bartender dated the man's daughter for over a year. She was hot, too."

With that, Bobby was off.

Adam smiled and took a sip of his drink. He pulled a pen from his pocket, a cocktail napkin from the pile and wrote: One for the book.

Bobby was back a few minutes later. Refilling Adam's glass, he motioned to the *One for the book* napkin sitting on the bar. "Here's a few more. Write this down."

Adam did as he was told and picked up his pen.

"Sights to see–or maybe you don't want to see– at a bar: one, a middle aged woman drinking Blue Moon chased with a Jäger Bomb... what a waste of Blue Moon.

Two, anyone drinking a Washington Apple... what a waste of Crown Royal. Three, a drunk old lady sucking face with a young buck... what a waste in general."

Bobby let out a loud laugh and was off again.

Adam smiled and added to his notes, "What's a Washington Apple?"

*****

Adam and Bobby watched as Phillip, one of the bar-backs, washed up a load of glasses. Conveniently, he was doing so in front of a young blonde. While she certainly wasn't the most attractive tree in the orchard, she certainly had nice peaches, which were covered in a tight yellow t-shirt for anyone interested to see. The two men continued to watch in silence, Bobby with a slight smile on his face, Adam with more of an expression of curiosity, wondering how far this glass-washing-peach-picking was going to go.

Bobby leaned forward so he could be heard above the noise. "The kid's working hard, but really for naught."

"What makes you say that?" Adam asked.

"He's been working on her for two weeks now, and he doesn't even have her number yet. She keeps telling him her phone is broke."

"Maybe it is."

Bobby chuckled. "When's the last time you saw a girl her age without a cell phone stuck in her ear? She'd be lost without it." He laughed again. "It's a new world out there, Adam... a brave new world."

"I guess it is," Adam said. "So why does he keep talking to her?"

"At the moment, he has no alternative. His girl dumped him a couple weeks ago. He told me she was jealous of him talking to other girls while he was working."

"Jealously, huh?"

"A deadly virus in this business," Bobby said. "The girl... the ex that is... was in love with him. Only in this business, there's no such thing as love, only lust."

"Why's that?"

"Too easy to be unfaithful. High stress, high pace, and when you mix opportunity with alcohol... hell, it's tough. We've talked before about this."

"Tough maybe, but not impossible," Adam suggested..

Bobby shrugged his shoulders. "An impossible dream."

The two men continued to watch over the orchard.

Adam's attention was distracted by the pressure of Mel's leg up against his. She looked at him and smiled. "You okay?" she asked.

"I'm fine... you?"

She nodded as the leg pressure intensified a bit.

"You have a cell phone?" Adam asked.

She laughed. "Yeah, why?"

Adam hesitated. "Can I have your number sometime?"

She winked at him. "My cell phone's broken." She watched Adam blush before continuing. "But when I get it back..."

*****

For whatever reason, the temperature inside Smitty McGee's was higher than normal. Adam suspected Sunny had yet to get the thermostats adjusted properly as the winter temperatures continued to fluctuate wildly. Regardless, the warmth didn't seem to sway the patrons from having a good time. The music was loud. The atmosphere was festive, and everyone seemed to be in a good mood. Adam estimated there was about a 50/50 mix of regulars verses newbies. Feeling in a pretty good mood himself, he sipped his drink, kept one eye on Mel who was playing Buzztime and another eye on the happenings around him.

On this particular night, it wasn't what he saw that was of interest, but rather what he was hearing. He sat quietly. He listened. He counted. He was in awe. He had heard it before, but had never paid it much mind. Tonight, however, it seemed to be even more prevalent than normal. In the last sixty seconds, it was used as a verb, an adjective and even a noun. In the last sixty seconds he had heard it at least ten times. He knew it was at least ten times because he ran out of fingers during the count. It was so versatile, he chuckled. What amazed him the most, however, was the casualness with which it was used in normal routine conversation–by men and by women. Sure, it was around while he was growing up, but it was one of those things kept for special moments in life, usually when you wanted to impress your buddies that you were cool. But in today's society, it was a part of normal conversation. It was a brave new world, all right!

He lifted his glass and emptied the last finger of

V.O. He turned and looked toward Mel, who was being announced on the screen as the winner of the game just concluded. A small charge ran down his spine ending at his tailbone. She was so smart, so beautiful, so kind.

He looked away before the electrical shock caused any further reaction. His stare went into empty space. He heard it several more times. He began to wonder if it was there before, but never noticed. True, he had trained in an inner city hospital, he had traveled to many countries, he had experienced many cultures and had seen many things. But had he really paid attention? Had he always been so focused on the task at hand–the next class to get to, the next test to study for, the next patient to see, the next plane to catch, the next surgery to perform–that he missed things like this. Had he missed out on life itself? He did have his time with Nancy, and that was wonderful, but had they both lived in a glass menagerie, so caught up in his career and in each other?

And now...

The moment before electrical charge was re-placed by a cloud of sadness. It was a cloud he had experienced before. Taking in a deep breath, he let the air out slowly. The cloud slowly faded.

He brought his thoughts back to the original topic at hand. He perked up his ears and started counting again. This time he ran out of fingers in less than thirty seconds. Again, there was a verb and an adjective, but this time he did not pick up a noun. A frown crossed his face. Maybe he had been living in a cocoon.

Bobby broke his train of thought as he set down a refill. The bartender saw the good doctor's mind was in la la land. Picking up the empty glass and cocking his head to the side, he said, "What the fuck are you in such deep thought about?"

Adam, who was about to take a sip of the fresh drink, stared hard at his newfound -friend. Was that an adjective or an adverb, he wondered? Then he broke out into laughter.

12

New Year's 2009

Adam glanced at the TV directly in front of him. It was just after 1:00 am. All the major networks had broken away from their New Year's Eve coverage. This particular channel was running an old John Wayne movie. That was fine, except the sound was turned down as rock music blared from the ceiling speakers. It amazed Adam that people would sit at a bar, sometimes for hours on end, and watch a television they could not hear.

He took a sip of his drink and looked at Mel, who was playing Buzztime. He watched her a moment, then turned his attention to a few stragglers who were preparing to leave. He hoped that whoever was the designated driver was already in the car. If not, he had no doubt Sunny had a cab standing by.

It had been a good night, a good crowd. For the most part, everyone was well behaved. Bobby only had to leap over the bar once to get in between two women who were arguing over, of all things, a bar stool. Another stool was quickly found, beers were refilled and peace was restored. Adam could tell by the expression on Bobby's face when the two women checked out that he was well rewarded for his peace keeping efforts. Mel, who had also witnessed the event, attributed the large tip to Bobby's leaping over the bar skills as much as his actual peace keeping ability. To see Bobby play Superman was enough to stop the most intense conversation, friendly or not.

Yes, it had been a good night, a fun night. Mel and Adam each arrived around 9:00–their agreed upon time–and thanks to some maneuvering by Bobby, were able to sit together. Time passed quickly. Mel sipped her wine. Adam was careful with his drink as Bobby passed by frequently, often with a bottle of V.O. in hand. They ate, too–wings, killer nachos, more wings, plus some other appetizers Sunny put out as the midnight hour approached. He and Mel talked, they laughed, and they intermingled with others doing the same. There were no special activities this evening. If it weren't for the decorations, the champagne toast at midnight, and the fact that people were dressed up more than usual, including the band, you wouldn't have known it was any different from any other evening.

There was one moment, however. It was during the first couple of minutes after midnight when handshakes and hugs were being distributed. Adam suddenly found himself face to face with

Mel. Time seemed to stand still. In spite of the noise in the air, an eerie silence engulfed them. There was a moment's hesitation. Mel leaned into him, and he did the same. Their lips were about to meet when Bobby arrived with more champagne and a slap on Adam's back. He leaned over and gave Mel a kiss on the cheek. "Happy New Year," he shouted above the noise of the crowd. Then, this time carrying a champagne bottle, he was gone. So was the moment. The band started playing *Auld Lang Syne.* Soon, everyone was singing, Adam and Mel included.

That was over an hour ago, and now the celebration was winding down. Bobby had sent the bar staff home and Sunny was just finishing up in the kitchen. The few remaining stragglers headed out the door. Comments were overheard that if they hurried, they still had time to find someplace to party in Maryland.

The lights went off in the kitchen. The house lights were dimmed. The music was turned down a few decibels. Sunny bid them farewell and left through the back door. Now, only Bobby, Mel and Adam remained. Bobby locked the door and came over to refill their drinks. He popped himself a cold Heineken and pulled out a stool that had been hiding in the corner most of the night. He held up his bottle. "Cheers."

"Cheers."

"Happy New Year."

"Happy New Year."

Silence followed as beverages were consumed. "Looks like you had a good night," Adam said, sitting his glass down.

Bobby shrugged his shoulders. "Pretty much as expected. Delaware bars have a tough time competing on New Year's because we close at 1:00 and Maryland stays open late. But I'm not complaining."

"Sunny seemed happy."

Bobby laughed. "Yeah, no one called out. Then again, she promised everyone who showed up a hundred dollar bonus and anyone who called out a pink slip."

Adam laughed, too.

Bobby stepped away and came back with bottles of B&B and wine. As another toast was made, his voice softened. "Anyway, tonight's the night."

"Huh?" Adam said, halfway through his shot.

"Tonight, we tell each other our stories."

Adam's eyes widened.

Bobby quickly continued. "You said you'd tell me yours when I told you mine. What better way to start the New Year than to get the cards out on the table? Clear conscience and all that stuff."

"I have a clear conscience," Adam spouted.

Bobby leaned forward. "Maybe a clear conscience isn't the correct wording. Maybe debunking the burden you've been carrying around for heaven only knows how many months is a better way of putting it." He pulled a quarter from his pocket. "We'll let chance decide. Your call." He tossed the coin skyward.

"Heads," Adam said instinctively.

Bobby caught the coin and slapped it on the bar. He moved his hand away. "Heads it is," he announced. "You go first."

Adam looked at the coin and then up at the bartender. His thoughts were interrupted by Mel. "Maybe I'd better go," she said.

Adam's and Bobby's eyes locked together. "Still your call," Bobby said.

Next to what he inevitably knew was about to happen, Mel's leaving was the last thing Adam wanted. He turned toward her. "Stay... please."

She looked at Bobby who smiled and said, "You still got half a glass of wine to finish."

She grinned sheepishly and repositioned herself on the stool.

Adam's drink was refilled as was the shot of B&B. He stared down at the bar and subconsciously downed half of his V.O.

"Anytime now," Bobby said encouragingly.

Adam made eye contact with the bartender before looking away. His shoulders slumped forward as he let out a sigh. "Yes, I am a pediatric neurosurgeon... one who has performed hundreds of operations on kids all over the world. Sometimes I've helped them, sometimes not. And yes, where I've really made my mark is in the field of conjoined or Siamese twins. I have written extensively on the subject as well. My work, and the lecturing that goes along with it, has allowed me to travel to places I've never even heard of before." Adam took a sip of his whisky. "However, all this fame and fortune came with a price. You see, I had a wonderful wife–a wife who stood behind me with everything I did. We were high school sweethearts; we went through undergraduate school at Hopkins together. I was in premed. She was a physical therapist. She was also an artist–a pretty good one, too."

"What kind of art did she do?" Mel asked.

"Paintings mostly. She was what you would call an impressionist."

"You said she was good. Was she successful?" Bobby injected.

"In local circles, yes. But she always said it was a hobby, and didn't want to get to where she had to paint."

"I can understand that," Mel said.

Adam continued. "Anyway, when we finished undergraduate school, she worked while I went to medical school. It was tough, but we made do. I must say, selling some of her paintings helped. During this time, all she ever asked was that when we could afford it, we'd start a family. Initially, she traveled everywhere with me. When she did get pregnant, we decided it would be best if she stayed home. In the meantime, I continued to tour the world–lecturing and operating at a high pace, even by Hopkins's standards. My fame grew. Her belly grew. It was a hectic time. As much as I wanted to be home with my wife, the demands of my practice dictated otherwise. As so often happens with people like myself, you lose the ability to say no."

"Then the Mohabee twins were born in Tanzania, Africa. That's just south of Kenya, directly on the equator. Hot as hell there, too." Adam took another sip of his drink. "Anyway, the twins were connected at the head, and shared parts of the same brain. Otherwise, they were healthy and developing normally. As such, they were excellent surgical candidates. Unfortunately, the government refused to issue travel visas–something to do with the political beliefs of the father. They also wanted to demonstrate to the world that they had high quality health care, which was really a ruse, considering we transported the entire team and most of the equipment over there. All they supplied was the space and the electricity."

As Adam continued, his eyes started to tear. "We did the case in less than eighteen hours–one of the faster we've ever done. It's really something to see a pair of conjoined twins look at each other for the first time. I came away from the case feeling really good, ready to tell the parents and the world that everything went okay."

Adam turned and looked directly at Bobby. By

now, tears were pouring down his cheeks. "Only that's not how it played out. While I was halfway around the world adding yet another feather to my cap, my wife was home when she suddenly became short of breath. She called a friend who came and took her to the ER at Hopkins. She died a short time later from a pulmonary embolism–a blood clot to the lung. When she died, so did our baby."

He looked away and wiped his arm across his face. When he looked back, his expression had an angry hue about it. "The best Goddamn hospital in the world couldn't save her, and I was thousands of miles away..." His eyes dropped down to his drink. He emptied both glasses. He felt Mel's arm up on his shoulder. Her fingers gently dug into the muscles. Her free hand wiped her own tears away.

As a final word, Adam added, "I came down here right after the funeral. I haven't been back since."

Except for the music overhead, the room was silent.

The silence was short lived as Bobby, who had been leaning forward and listening intently, straightened up. "Heavy bars, man. Heavy bars." He refilled the empty glasses and added some wine to Mel's goblet. He held up his own shot. "What was your wife's name?"

Adam looked at him a moment. "Nancy... her

name was Nancy."

"How about the baby?"

"We hadn't picked a name yet."

"Fine," Bobby said. "Here's to Nancy and Baby Singer." He downed his drink. Mel took a sip of her wine, a much larger sip than normal. Adam took a little longer, but the shot glass was returned to the bar in an empty state.

"Heavy bars," Bobby repeated.

Another period of silence passed, and then Bobby said, "Well, I guess we'd better get out of here before the sun comes up.

He started to walk away but was stopped by Adam, who reached out and grabbed his arm. "Not so fast," the doctor commanded. Bobby turned and looked at Adam, a quizzical expression on his face. "It's your turn," Adam said.

"My turn?"

"Yeah, I went first. Now it's your turn."

Bobby laughed nervously. "It's kind of late." He looked over at Mel.

She tapped the side of her glass and said, "I still have half a glass."

"But..."

Adam picked up the quarter that was still sitting on the bar. "We'll let chance decide. Call it in the air." He tossed the quarter skyward.

"Tails," Bobby said.

Adam caught the coin and slapped it down with a thud. "Tails," he announced as he pulled his hand away. "You lose. Start talking." He reached over, grabbed the bottle of B&B and refilled the two empty shot glasses. Emptying his own, he said, "Anytime now."

A dumbfounded look on his face, Bobby again glanced over at Mel, who herself didn't know whether to continue crying or break out into laughter. She did neither, instead raising her own glass in a toast. "Anytime now," she mimicked.

Bobby looked back at Adam. A thin smile formed. "You know Doc, you're a lot smarter than you look... and..." He emptied his own shot. "There's hope for you yet." He sat back down on the stool. The smile faded. He looked at the two bar patrons. "Mel here knows my story, so I'll keep it brief." He took a sip of beer. "In my younger days, I was a cop... an Ocean City cop to be precise. For the most part, it was an easy gig. Most of what I did was write parking tickets and deal with drunken teenagers. However, it didn't pay squat. The first couple years there was plenty of overtime, but then the new mayor came along and the budget ax came out. Overtime was cut way back. So I had to find something else to supplement my income. I looked around and saw that the town was always in need of wait staff and bartenders. I figured I'd rather be serving up booze than food. I knew the owner of the Clarion Hotel, as most cops knew the owners of the businesses in town. So I pulled him over one day for running a green light and threatened to give him a ticket if he didn't teach me the bar trade. I argued it would be good for him in that he would get a free security guard at the same time. He was known for his sense of humor, so he agreed. It was a good place to work in that the clients were usually older and more subdued–didn't have all the drunkenness like we get around here sometimes."

"So things were good–that is until my sister..." He paused. "My sister dabbled in drugs all her life, although she was never a hard core druggie. She did, however, like the money that dealing brought in. She'd been in trouble with the law a couple times over the years, but always found a way to stay out of jail. The last time, however..." He paused again, taking a sip of beer. "Well, let's just say she did it up good. The feds raided her house... it's just down the street a bit... and found a shit pile of marijuana and several thousand dollars worth of cocaine. Since this was her third offense, they threw the book at her. They gave her a plea bargain of eight years with five years minimum before chance of parole. Since she was looking at over thirty years if found guilty on all charges, she took the deal. She really had no choice." This time Bobby took a long swig of beer.

"How did that affect you?" Adam asked.

Bobby chuckled. "Besides living in the house–it

was our mother's–I was actually there at the time of the raid." His tone turned serious. "But her three kids were in the house, too. It was a real nightmare." He paused. "One of the things my sister did as part of the plea bargain was to insist I was totally innocent and knew nothing about her activity, which was actually the case. Still, it didn't look good for a cop to be in a house that was raided by the feds. So it was recommended that I resign from the force, which I did without question, knowing full well that if I didn't, they'd find another way to get rid of me. I quit the department, left the Clarion and ended up here, where I can walk to work and be a lot closer to the animals."

"The animals?" Adam queried.

"My niece and two nephews. They're cute, but they are wild."

Adam remembered the day he took a stroll down to Bobby's house. "You're raising the three kids by yourself?" Adam also remembered that besides Bobby and the three kids, someone else was there that day.

Bobby nodded towards Mel. "Mel, here, is like a sister to me. We all grew up together. She's a real dear and helps out when she can. But yes, officially, they're all mine."

"He's doing a wonderful job with them, too," Mel chimed in.

"Some days I think I am; other days I wonder,"

Bobby said.

"No other relatives?" Adam asked.

"Both our parents are dead. The kids' father is a deadbeat somewhere down in Florida. As far as any other relatives, there's none I could trust, or who would even be interested. So it was me or social services." He looked away. "I saw a couple foster care cases go bad when I was on the force, so there was really no decision to be made. My sister signed custody over to me the day she signed the plea bargain."

"He works his ass off for those children," Mel said.

"We do okay," Bobby insisted. He drained his beer.

Adam emptied his own glass. "Heavy bars," he said.

Bobby nodded in agreement. He held up the empty bottle in a toast. "Happy New Year, you two."

"Happy New Year," Adam and Mel said in unison.

*****

After a final round of drinks, and making sure the lights were out and doors locked, the trio made their way out to the parking lot. Mel offered to take Bobby home, but he declined, suggesting her time would be better served making sure someone else got home safely. Mel gave him a *would you please behave* look. In return, he gave her a wink and told her to have fun. Nodding to Adam, he turned and headed toward his street. Mel insisted on taking Adam home, arguing that there were too many crazy drivers out tonight for him to be walking along Route 54. Besides, a chilling breeze had come up the past couple of hours, making the decision easier. Except for Adam giving Mel directions and a comment about the sobriety check points they heard about earlier, they rode the mile and a half in silence.

As Mel pulled into the driveway and put her SUV in park, Adam turned to her and said, "I just want to tell you I had a really good time tonight."

"I did too."

Adam looked toward the house. A single porch light illuminated the otherwise dark structure. The view stimulated the same feeling he had been experiencing the past few weeks whenever returning home late. He wondered if that was the why behind his spending so much time at the bar lately. He definitely vacillated through a spectrum of feelings over the past months–some good, some bad. Encompassing all these, however, was the one he deemed the most distressing... the most dangerous. And that was loneliness. It was like a vulture overhead, waiting for the opportunity to strike.

Looking at Mel, he could see her face in the faint glow of the light. He was mesmerized the first time he saw her. That feeling had only grown stronger which only added to the pain... the grief... the loneliness–all feelings that were new to him since Nancy...

He cut the thought off as a wave of sadness *tsunamied* him. He spoke softly. "As far as..."

Mel leaned over, put her finger across his lips and gave him a kiss on the cheek. "You don't have to explain. I understand. Go get some sleep. Maybe I'll see you later. We can have a bowl of chili or something." She handed him a card from the shop. "Let me know if you need a ride. My cell phone number's on the back."

He smiled. "You got it fixed?"

She nodded.

Adam watched as she backed out of the drive-way and headed down the street. She turned the corner and her lights disappeared. He continued to stare in that direction. For the first time in a long time he felt regret for a decision he made. He even contemplated going after her, but he knew that would be wasted energy. He looked at the card in his hand. He had a number, but no address.

He turned and walked toward the house, the porch light drawing him in like a mosquito in the summer. The sadness continued. He cursed himself for going into Smitty McGee's the first time.

He cursed himself for even getting a haircut that day. He should have continued his walk like he did every day. So what if his hair was long? So what if he got caught out in the rain? Why did he go and screw up his routine? After all, he was surviving by minimizing his life, which minimized the pain–surviving life without a life. Now, he had come out the cave and look where it got him. The pain was no longer minimal. Other feelings were running wild. Talking about Nancy only made things worse. So why did he do it? Why did he let Bobby manipulate him into telling his story? He should have been more cautious. He should have had more sense. He should have...

"Stop it!" he said aloud, so loud he looked around to make sure no one else was outside. He quickly went into the house.

Before, when he was home, he was alone in his own little world, protected from the past by the emptiness of surroundings, the emptiness of his emotions, the emptiness of his life. But that had all changed tonight with a flip of a coin. He cursed Bobby under his breath. He went to his recliner and sat down. He stared out the patio door into the darkness. He closed his eyes and wished his mind to go blank. Only, it refused to obey. Instead, thoughts continued to kaleido-scope through his mind... thoughts, ideas, emotions he had not addressed in a long time.

He cursed Bobby again, this time much louder.

New Year's Day 2009

The first sunrise of the new year found the temperature in the mid-50s. While the sun was trying to warm the air, there was still a noticeable chill. Figuring the fresh air would do him good, Adam took his coffee out and sat on the back deck. For the moment, the wind was calm, the sky scattered with clouds. He stared across the empty lots towards the water. Unlike the week before, the lots were now outlined with stakes sporting little red ribbons. The remaining breeze from the night before was enough to flutter the ribbons back and forth. It was a subtle change in the landscape, and the meaning was significant. The property had been surveyed. Property surveyed meant the lot had been sold and the building of a house would begin soon. His view out across the water would be compromised–a view he had come to depend on as a way of passing the time. It was his emotional hibernation, his analgesic for the pain.

A chill went up his spine as a gust of wind blew by. He hunched his shoulders and pulled the collar up on his jacket. He took a sip of coffee and waited for the warmth to take effect. He scanned the area, imprinting the image into his mind. Maybe when the view was gone, he would still be able to see it with his eyes closed. A bird came into view. It circled twice before landing high up in one of the tallest trees. It sat there looking for its next meal, its head turning in sharp snapping movements. Adam stared at the water and wait-ed. Today, however, instead of the normal trance, his mind continued to swirl. Thoughts scrolled across his mind like words across a computer screen. He closed his eyes, trying to ignore the images... the words... the letters. His efforts failed. Finally, he let things come into focus.

HEAVY BARS... HEAVY BARS...

The scrolling continued, and with it came addi-tional words... additional thoughts... old memories... recent memories... memories from the night before.

It started out as a pleasant evening. Time spent at Smitty McGee's seemed to be that way. Then once everybody left, a coin was tossed and things changed. Thoughts, images, memories... issues he had managed to keep buried these months suddenly rose to the surface. Why did he let Bob-by do this to him? He should have kept the past to himself, buried where it belonged. Why couldn't Smitty's just be a place to go, to get a bite to eat, a drink or two, and...

His thoughts stumbled. He rewound a few steps. Have a drink or two–hibernate in a differ-ent fashion, without the loneliness perhaps. Still, why did Bobby have to question him, pick on him, pry into his life? Why couldn't Adam just be left alone, another figure at the bar whose story was unknown? Why did he let his book be opened?

Then there was the whole issue with Mel. She had come into his life, bringing forth additional emotions. Yet, she had done nothing to him but cut his hair and be a friend. She never pressed him for information, for affection, for anything. Even last night after they spent the whole evening together–New Year's Eve no less–they parted ways without so much as a kiss good night. She may have wanted it. She may have offered with her eyes. But she certainly did not press him. She said she understood. But how could she? How could anyone?

He took in a deep breath. The wave of anger slowly ebbed. The normal sadness mixed with a dose of loneliness returned. The trees in the distance swayed back and forth in response to the gentle breeze. "How could she understand?" Adam repeated, this time aloud. Yet, she said she did. The anger started to return. Tears filled his eyes. He wiped them away with a cold sleeve. There was no way. A pessimistic wave flowed over him. He started to curse Bobby yet again, but the idea was cut short. He suddenly realized there were three people at the bar last night and only two stories were told. Was the answer there somewhere?

He focused back on the scene before him. While

he had his doubts, there was also a hint of hope.

New Year's evening

Bobby topped off Mel's glass of wine–her third of the evening. There was obviously something bothering her and Bobby had little doubt what it was. Recorking the bottle, Bobby said, "Don't worry, I suspect your boyfriend will be here soon."

"My boyfriend!" She stared him hard in the eye. "As you are well aware, Robert, I do not have a boyfriend... except you that is." Her facial expression softened as she blew him a kiss. "I'm worried about him, Bobby. Last night may have been a bit much"

"It's okay to worry," Bobby said. "Just not too much. You may not think so, but Adam there, he's a tough guy. It'll take time, but he'll come around."

"Come around! When?"

Bobby looked past Mel, a thin smile forming on his face. "Say in about five seconds." His smiled widened.

Mel sensed the presence of someone behind her. She turned just in time to see Adam slide up on the bar stool next to her. She resisted the urge to give him a big hug and kiss.

"Evening, Adam. How you feeling today?" Bobby said, wiping off the bar in front of his newest customer.

"Fine, thanks. How about you?"

"Nothing a couple aspirin this morning didn't cure." Bobby stepped away to fetch a bottle of V.O.

Adam turned towards Mel. "And you?"

Mel smiled, a sense of warmth engulfing her. "I'm fine, thanks. I'm glad you stopped by."

"We had a date, didn't we?"

Mel's mouth opened. The hint of a blush followed.

Adjusting his stool, Adam pulled a quarter from his pocket and flipped it in the air. He smacked his hand over it as the silver piece struck the bar. "Heads," he announced.

"Huh?" Mel, said.

"It's your turn."

"For what?"

"What's your story, Mel?" Adam said. "And don't tell me you don't have one because you would have never said *I understand* unless..." He stopped and watched the color drain from her face. It was not the reaction he was expecting. He looked to Bobby for support, but the bartender was already heading toward a foursome that had just come through the far door. By the time he refocused on Mel, tears were already forming. "I'm sorry, I didn't mean to..."

A finger came up across his lips. "It's okay," Mel said. "You're right, no one can fully understand how someone else feels. They may be able to understand a little and maybe more if..." She drank the rest of her wine. "You want the short version or the long one?"

"Whatever you want," Adam said, struggling to fend off the guilt he was suddenly feeling.

She turned and stared blankly across the bar. "My husband was in the military, the Marines to be specific. He was the true blue soldier, full of vigor, full of spirit, full of love for his country–a true patriot if there ever was one. He was in Iraq in the early days, even before the first war officially started. He'd write me, tell me he was in the desert, tell me how much he loved and missed me, and tell me it was hot as hell. He couldn't tell me what he was doing, except that he was playing Marine." Mel paused. "He was one of the first ones to go into Iraq. He was also one of the first ones home. Only..." She turned and looked at Adam. "He came home in a wooden box, Adam. The love of my life, my childhood sweetheart just like you, left me on two feet and came home eighteen months later flat on his back covered in an American flag." Her eyes teared. "I don't know how you heard about your wife, but when I looked out the window that morning and saw an unmarked car pulling into my driveway, I knew."

"Oh, my God," Adam said.

"My words exactly."

*****

The rest of the night followed the normal script of an evening at the bar. Glasses up and down the bar were refilled, emptied and refilled again. An occasional round of shots was thrown in for good luck. Food was served–the most popular of the night was beef au jus. Bobby claimed it was the best hangover food on the menu. The Orange Bowl continued in silence, the commentators drowned out by the sounds of Alice Cooper blaring from the speakers. The crowd was sparse, yet jovial. Most of the younger conversation dealt with what happened to whom, who drank what and who ended up with whom at the end of the night. The older crowd talked football, and about the weather. Winter at the beach was the same every day–cold, windy and cloudy. Coffee was kept fresh and the evening ticked away.

Except to keep their glasses filled and to share a shot of B&B, Bobby left Mel and Adam alone. The foursome from earlier continued to keep the bartender busy as they were now trying a variety of cocktails, some they ordered by name, others Bobby suggested. Adam did mention to Mel that he had yet to see their designated driver arrive. To which Mel replied that Adam shouldn't worry as she suspected Bobby already had their car keys in his pocket. "They don't come in here often," Mel went on to explain. "When they do, they get so sloshed they can hardly walk out. It's nothing for them to run up a several hundred dollar bar tab, so Bobby and Sunny see that they get back to their condo safely."

"That's nice of them," Adam said.

"Nice and good for business," Mel said. "They can't spend money if they're dead alongside the road."

Adam tipped his head to the side at the crassness of her comment. In spite of all the softness she conveyed, her shell was pretty hard. Then again, she had been married to a Marine... a Marine who was now...

He let the thought go unfinished as he realized there was still a lot about her he didn't know.

While Adam watched the people, Mel played Buzztime. During breaks in the game, they talked a little, nothing of substance, however. There was an air of tension between them, yet there also seemed to be a newly formed bond, an understanding, a realization that while they may not each be in the same boat, they were in boats nonetheless, floating around aimlessly, looking for... searching for...

"For what?" Adam said aloud.

Mel turned to him. "What did you say, honey?"

"Nothing," he said, embarrassed.

She gave him a smile and returned to her game.

146

Yes, there was tension. And yes, there was a new bond. For the first time in a long time he felt as if a weight had been lifted off his shoulders. It was as if he could see again, hear again, feel again. For the first time, he was really out of his cave, out of his hibernation.

And, in spite of his earlier emotions, it felt good.

Nothing had changed concerning his feelings toward Nancy. Nothing had changed concerning the pain he felt. Yet...

The bars were still there, yet he could now at least see around them. He was feeling pain and happiness, both at the same time.

Was that possible, he wondered. It was a question to consider carefully.

In the meantime, his glass was empty. He looked around for Bobby. He needed another drink.

At the moment, country music (versus the usual rock and roll) was blaring out across the speaker system. Country music meant one thing–Sunny had arrived. It was a rule among the staff that whoever saw her come in first would change the radio to one of the country stations in the area. Sunny would come in, hear it, and change it back to a rock channel. It was the signal the boss had arrived.

Adam picked up the change in music, but he ignored it for the moment. He was trying hard not to let what had started out as a pleasant day turn bad. He was also scolding himself for being so stupid... so crass for forcing Mel's hand. He should have known better. He should have had more... more compassion.

Bobby buzzed by and saw the expressions on the two faces. He came to an abrupt halt, did an about face and returned a moment later with bottles in hand. All glasses refilled, he raised his own shot in the air and said, "In the journey of life, one should never ask a question if not prepared for all possible answers. At the same time, one should never answer said question if not prepared for the emotions such a discussion might bring forth."

The shots were downed and the two glasses quickly slid beneath the bar as Sunny was now in the house.

Mel said, "You know Bobby, sometimes I wonder what people around here would do without you."

Adam chuckled. "I was kind of wondering what we were going to do with him."

Bobby stared at him a moment. "Did I just witness the good doctor here crack a joke?" Adam blushed. Mel smiled.

"There's hope for you yet, Adam," Bobby said. He headed toward an empty glass he spotted a few seats away.

Adam looked at Mel. "I'm sorry," he said.

"There's nothing to be sorry about," she said.

Adam continued. "Not the best way to start off a new year. Between last night and today..."

Mel leaned toward him. He met her half way. "On the other hand, maybe it is," Mel said.

Adam hesitated before putting his arm around her waist. He drew her in closer. "You ready for that bowl of chili?"

Her head dropped to his shoulder. "Sounds good."

*****

One of the regulars sitting three or four stools down from Adam, said, "Hey, what did the guy who jumped off the empire state building say to the people on each floor as he passed by?"

"What did he say?" someone responded.

"So far, so good."

Bobby laughed and turned his attention to Adam. "Here's one for the book," he said. "A guy asks a bartender for a beer and a pack of matches and throws a $50.00 bill on the bar."

"Expensive matches," Adam commented.

"Not if the matches are full of cocaine."

Later in the same night, Adam noticed a crooked tarnished spoon hanging over one of the beer taps. He had been watching for over an hour, and this particular tap had been used several times, yet the spoon had not been touched. It just hung there, balanced like a circus acrobat, waiting its turn to enter the ring. Adam's question: what act would the spoon perform? Days later, the question of the spoon's purpose would still be unanswered.

When Adam asked Bobby about this on one occasion, the bartender responded by saying that there are many questions in life that go unanswered.

13

Mid-January 2009

Winter continued its grasp on the area. Snow had fallen the day before and covered the ground. The wind blew off the ocean, sending a chill through anyone who happened outside for too long. It was a rare time in history when there was absolutely no one on the 2¾ mile stretch of the Ocean City Boardwalk for hours on end. The sky was overcast, as the storm, while finished with its snow dump phase, was still making its way out of the region. To ride down Coastal Highway, one got a sense of a deserted town. But that was only an illusion. For you see, everyone who normally would have been outside roaming about was tucked away somewhere at their favorite watering hole. It was a winter Monday night, and that meant one thing–Monday night football.

Bobby came by with a refill and a basket of wings. Setting the food down in front of Adam, he said, "You like football?"

"Can't say I'm a hardcore fan, but I do like it once in a while."

"Well, you're a better man than me," Bobby said. He slid the wings towards Adam. "Screw up in the kitchen, so enjoy."

Adam looked at the wings. "What was the screw up?" He picked up a wing and directed it towards his mouth.

Bobby laughed. "We got a new line cook in the back who doesn't know the difference between mild and hot."

Adam was just about to take a bite when his hand lowered a few inches. "Which way did the screw up go?"

Bobby laughed. "You tell me." And he was off.

It was a good fifteen minutes before the bartender returned to the scene. Clearing away the basket and several balled up napkins, he said, "So?"

Adam, whose glass of V.O. was empty, as was a glass of water sitting beside it, said, "I'd say your new line cook doesn't know the difference between mild and super-hot."

Bobby laughed and looked into the empty basket. "Didn't seem to stop you none."

"Once I got past the first inferno, it wasn't too bad."

Bobby chuckled again. "I'll tell the new guy you liked 'em."

"You do that," Adam said, turning his attention back to the game.

February 2009

It was a chilly February night. Half the staff had already had the flu. The other half was showing the signs of succumbing soon. Adam was a little worried in that he had not had the appropriate vaccination. He mentioned this to Bobby who shrugged his shoulders and said, "what will be will be." He did, however, return a few minutes later with two B&B's. Sliding one to the doctor, he said, "This ought to solve your problem."

"How's that?" Adam said, downing the liquid.

"Flu shot."

*****

A Valentine's Day Poem

Roses are red.
Violets are blue.
Damn, I'm so fucking
In love with you.

*****

As winter continued, Adam realized that except for the seasonal decorations, the place itself changed very little. There continued to be some turnover of kitchen and wait staff. The bartenders, however, remained fixed. Doug, who had been there the longest, was working on his eighth year–a long time in this business. Bobby was in his fifth. Everyone else had been there at least two, the exception being a couple of other part-timers.

The core base of regular customers remained the same as well. There were faces Adam saw almost every time he came in, and there were faces that if he didn't see this time, they'd surely be there the next. Mixed with this were the semi-regulars as well as the newbies. The conversation among patrons was always easy and light, the exception being if the topic turned to politics or sports. Weather, fishing, the economy, families... whatever floated one's boat at any particular moment was fair game. People listened and nodded, and patiently waited their turn to say something. After all, no one was in a hurry, and there were noticeably no clocks around to indicate just how long someone had been sitting at the bar.

Among the regulars, there was often talk about each other, especially when the person of interest was absent. Nothing was ever done maliciously, but the regulars could stab each other in the back with the best of `em. Adam grew fond of listening to these particular conversations. For one, in reality, it was mindless banter amongst friends. For another, it did give him a feel for the true personalities that frequented the bar. He also reckoned it was somewhat representative of the people in the community in general. After a while, he realized the people at Smitty's were no different from anywhere else. Life's soap opera was the same, regardless of which channel you watched it on.

Yes, they did talk about people behind their backs. They also had little hesitation about doing the same right to your face. On this particular night, the crowd was sparse. Ricky was playing a ballad he had written years before. As the majority of the patrons were men versus women (eleven to one to be precise), the conversation focused on who had the best legs. Sunny denied it, but Adam suspected it was a requirement for employment. Tall, short, skinny, a little robust–it didn't matter, as long as you had nice legs.

After twenty minutes of heated discussion and a couple rounds of shots, everyone's attention turned to Adam. "Hey, Adam," someone said. "Give us your opinion. Who has the best legs in here?"

That someone turned out to be a regular named George. He was an elderly waterman who made most of his money through the years buying and selling real estate. It was rumored he could have retired years ago, but his love for the water kept him going. When asked about this once, he responded by saying that real estate paid his bills and crabbing paid for his beer.

At the particular moment the question came his way, Adam had just taken a swig of his V.O. He held it in his mouth as an excuse not to talk immediately. He knew it was a loaded question as a couple of the young waitresses who were cleaning up for the night stopped their activity and looked in his direction. Sunny, who had also just come out of the kitchen, stopped to lend her ear to the conversation as well.

Adam swallowed and said, "Depends."

"Depends?" George the waterman said. "What the fuck kind of answer is that?" His words were slurred, indicating the cells in his brain were well sautéed.

"Just what I said," Adam defended. "It depends." He took a quick sip of his drink. "If you're asking purely for looks, I'd say Holly over there has a nice set." Holly was one of the two girls cleaning up. She was also the newest and the prettiest. "If you're looking for strength, then Julie." Julie was the other waitress. It was well known among the regulars that she was training for a marathon. She had the legs to show for it, too. "But I think at this particular moment," Adam continued, "I'd have to say Sunny there." He pointed in the direction of the owner.

George again started to question the answer, but Adam held up his hand and continued. "Sunny has the best legs because they're attached to feet that if you don't watch yourself, she's going to put one of them right up your ass."

The group broke into laughter. The waterman stared at Adam before glancing over at Sunny, who stood there leaning against the bar, her short legs crossed in front of her. "You want the right one or the left one, George?" she inquired.

George, while drunk, was not intoxicated to the point of stupidity, said, "Certainly sounds like the right answer to me."

And the band played on.

*****

Bobby pointed to a hot girl sitting at the far corner of the bar. She was talking to Sunny, laughing and joking, oblivious (presumably) to the activity going on around her, which consisted partially of the men at the bar staring at intervals. "See her?" Bobby said, "I saw her out on the beach one day and she had on one of those bikinis that drew the line between legal and nude beach. Anyway, she had a tattoo right above her ass that reads: *In the middle of a dream.* You know me, no couth, so I asked her what it meant. She smiled at me and said, 'If you're behind me looking down at my tattoo, you're in the middle of a dream.'"

Laughing at his own words, Bobby continued.

"Speaking of dreams, a guy meanders up to a pretty brunette who was sitting with a couple friends. The guy asks, 'Are your feet tired?' The girl gave him a questioning look. 'No, should they be?' 'Could be,' the guy nods. 'You've been running through my dreams all night.'"

As he laughed again, Bobby pulled a couple cocktail napkins from his pocket. Sliding them toward Adam, he said, "I've been making some notes for our book. Look them over and let me know what you think." He nodded and walked away.

Adam unfolded the papers and read:

1) Happiness isn't what you see in the mirror. It's what you see when you close your eyes.

2) Beer when the boss is here. Grand Marnier when she's not.

3) In the bar business, if you can give a back rub, you can get laid.

4) Life is full of people behind bars. The key is to find your cell mate... your soul mate.

A short time later, Bobby came by and dropped a couple of shots in front of Adam. The doctor looked at the glasses, noticed the liquid was clear and said, "What's this?"

"It ain't B&B."

"I can see that. What is it?"

"Vodka."

"Vodka... I don't do vodka."

"Tough shit. Drink it." The bartender lifted his

158

own glass and downed the liquor. He made a sour face and wiped his mouth with his arm.

Adam did the same, only his facial expression was much more prolific. Setting the glass down, he took a large swallow of V.O. His facial features tightened even more. "Jesus," he muttered. "Thanks for ruining the taste of V.O."

"You're welcome," Bobby said. "Sometimes in life you have to take a chance and try something different... something out of *your ordinary*. It takes time to get used to something different–like acquiring the taste of a new kind of booze. Know what I mean?" He didn't wait for an answer. He grabbed the two shot glasses and was off.

Adam stared after him, trying to make sense out of what Bobby just said. It was difficult, however, as the taste of vodka still permeated his senses. He did decide it would take him a *long* time to acquire the taste of vodka.

He spun around in his seat and looked toward the band. They were there in full force, making music, spreading the gospel of the *Bourbon Tabernacle Choir*. But there was something else that caught Adam's attention at this particular moment. The band was surrounded by flat screen TV's. And they were all on. ESPN, Buzztime, a fishing channel, the weather channel, and for whatever reason, one of the C Span channels was even on. Adam shook his head side to side as he thought: what an eclectic collection of channels.

He turned away before anyone noticed what he was doing. He looked up and down the bar. There was Doug. There was Bonnie, one of the new bartenders. There was Bobby. Sunny was even mixing a shaker of margaritas. Adam's smile widened. What an eclectic collection of bartenders. He didn't dare look at the people on his side of the bar.

*****

The crowd was especially noisy this night. The band, energized with several rounds of shots, did little to help the decibel level. Because they arrived late, Adam and Mel were forced to sit at the back end of the bar. Bobby sauntered by on one occasion with sweat beaded on his brow. "So how you two doing down here, tonight?" he asked.

"We're fine," Mel replied.

"Lively crowd tonight," Adam said.

"The DC gang is here, and they tend to get a bit noisy," Bobby explained.

"A bit!" Mel mocked.

"Yeah, but..."

"I know," Mel interrupted. "A three hundred dollar bar tab and a big tip."

Bobby gave her one of his grins. "You betcha." He wiped his arm across his forehead. "She was all over me again tonight," he said, referring to one of the ladies who traveled with the group.

"She wants you," Mel teased.

"She's married," Bobby reminded her.

Mel laughed. "When did that ever stop you?"

"Now, now my dear, you know I don't mess around with married women." Bobby looked over to where the group in question was gathering up their belongings. "They're probably going over to Ocean City."

"The night's young," Adam said, letting out a big yawn.

Bobby laughed. "She tried to kiss me once tonight and whispered in my ear that she'd been dreaming about me lately."

"I'd take that as a compliment," Mel said.

"I guess so. I sometimes wonder how far she'd really go."

"I wouldn't answer that question anytime soon," Mel recommended.

"I don't plan to." Bobby paused. "Got me to thinking though."

"About what it would be like to..."

Bobby cut Mel off. "No, not that. Just about dreams. We all have dreams in life, you know."

His curiosity raised, Adam said, "What are your dreams, Bobby?"

The bartender shrugged his shoulders. "Mainly that the kids grow up and stay healthy, and that my sister gets her shit together one of these days."

"Nothing else?"

Bobby pondered. "Well, I've always said I'd like to someday stand on a beach and watch the sun set in the ocean."

It took Adam a moment to figure that one out. He turned to Mel. "What about you, Mel, what dreams do you have?"

She laughed and blushed at the same time. "I always wanted to get my hair done by one of those high *falutin* Hollywood stylists." She instinctively ran her hand across her head.

"That's a good one," Adam said.

"What about you, Adam. What are your dreams?" Bobby countered.

Adam stared off into space. "I don't have any dreams anymore," he said solemnly.

"Bullshit!" Bobby responded. "You got dreams, Adam. You just don't recognize 'em."

"Well..."

Mel leaned over and placed her arm around his shoulder. "Sometimes you have to learn how to dream again," she said.

14

A few questions from Adam:

1) How many dollars does biker's week really put into the local economy?

2) And why do so many people object to this?

3) What is the best hangover food? (Not on the menu.)

4) What is it with people who come to the shore during the off season and go out to the beach regardless of the weather?

5) Why does the well put together St John designer woman go for the scruffy bearded biker dude?

Answers from Bobby:

1) A couple million.

2) They're idiots.

3) Orange juice and donuts.

4) They're idiots too.

5) $60,000 dollar vibrators.

*****

Adam watched as two middle aged men, from the somewhat regular category, sat glancing through one of those small plastic covered flip charts that told of specials and the upcoming events on the designated day of the week. They stopped on the Thursday page which talked about fifty cent oysters, three dollar burgers and the wine special for the evening. Not a big seller, the daily wine special did have its following. Today's special was a Merlot from one of the local wineries. Adam had already seen a couple of glasses poured.

Sliding the plastic flip chart aside, one of the young men said as he raised his beer to his mouth, "Who the fuck drinks wine at a bar anyway?"

As fate would have it, Sunny just happened to pass by. One of her hands was empty; the other was holding a glass of wine. She stopped in her tracks, pivoted so she was facing the two men, pushed up on her toes and said smartly, "You boys have a problem with people who drink wine?"

Both men turned red. Both stammered as they tried to come up with a response. "No ma'am," was the best they could do.

"Then shut the fuck up," Sunny snapped. She turned and walked away.

The crowd around the two men laughed. There was even scattered applause. The two smiled and nodded, acknowledging they had just had their butts whipped by one of the best. But before they could regroup and return to their own beverages of choice, Sunny returned. This time she had a smile on her face. She set two half-filled shot glasses in front of them. Her eyebrows rose as she spoke. "Never say no to anything before you taste it first." She gave them a flirting wink, turned and left again.

The wine samples were downed. A pair of ugly faces was made. More laughter followed. The two men returned to their beer. This time they kept their thoughts to themselves.

Later on the same evening the two men confirmed their newfound distaste for wine, a female newbie asked Sunny if they made orange crushes. Sunny said they made them, but not with real oranges. She insisted, however, they tasted the same and would she like to try one. The customer, a middle aged woman who was there with several of her peers declined the offer and ordered beers instead.

Adam heard this and turned to Mel, who had just arrived a few minutes before, "What's an orange crush?" he asked.

She leaned over and pressed her chest into his arm. Her actions surprised him. "It's a drink started by a place over in West Ocean City called Harborside," she said. "I'll take you there sometime."

"I'd like that," he acknowledged.

She remained pressed into him a couple more seconds. Their eyes met. Nothing else was said.

She blew him a gentle kiss and straightened up. He returned to his people watching task, she to her trivia. "An orange crush," he mouthed softly. Yes, he thought, he'd like to try one of those sometime.

Late February 2009

One evening while waiting for Mel to arrive, Adam caught himself staring at the display of Smitty McGee shirts. There were biker week shirts, St. Patty's Day attire and many just promoting the bar itself. The majority were laced with male appealing designs. One shirt in particular caught his eye. It was a well-proportioned babe holding a tray of raw oysters out in front of her body. The female caricature certainly had a lot to look at, but it was the caption beneath the design that caught Adam's eye.

Shuck, Suck, Swallow

Adam could only shake his head. It was a brave new world indeed.

Just then, Sunny strolled by. She stopped, wiped the area in front of him and said, "Evening, Adam. Bobby's tied up in the back stacking a delivery for me." She gave him a friendly wink. "There are some advantages to being short. Need anything?"

Adam looked past her and chuckled. "Yeah,

why don't you shuck me up a dozen oysters?"

She glanced over her shoulder in the direction of Adam's stare. Looking back, her smile widened. She went up on her toes and leaned forward. In a soft voice, she whispered, "We sell a lot of oysters with that shirt."

Then, like Bobby, she was gone.

*****

The person drawing Adam's attention was a short petite blonde sitting next to him. She arrived with two other similarly attractive female companions. They ordered beers and were talking and laughing amongst themselves. The girl appeared to be in her late 20s, maybe early 30s. Unlike her companions, who were dressed for the hunt, she was more conservative, sporting a white sweater and black slacks. She wore minimal make-up and simple pearl earrings.

Using the *occasional glance in that direction* technique, Adam gathered whatever information he could. His people watching skills had improved over the past few weeks, and the question rose, spearheaded by Bobby's lecturing: what was her story? He considered himself a good judge of character, a skill required when interviewing potential candidates for the few and highly coveted positions at Hopkins. But like most aspects of his profession, it was a skill that required practice–which was how he justified his clandestine behavior at the bar.

What was her story? From the tone of her voice together with her appearance and the way she handled herself in general, he labeled her as a hard working office-type girl who probably attended church on a regular basis and maybe even sang in the choir. That she was even out in a bar having a beer with friends he guessed was a rarity.

Yes, he decided as he took a sip of his drink, that was at least the foundation of her character.

That is until he overheard her say in a rather non-ladylike voice, "I was fuckin' mad. The bitch was about to slap me, only her old man grabbed her arm in time. Can you imagine?"

Adam tuned out the rest of the conversation, trying hard not to cough too loud as he cleared the liquor from his lungs. Reminding himself about Donny G, the military friend of Bobby's from several months before, Adam decided he'd better work harder on his people judging skills.

Deep in the inner layers of his brain, another question was born: what other skills was he losing?

Early March 2009

For the third time in as many minutes, Adam scanned the area around him. There was something different and it took him a while to realize what it was. Except for the TV's, the forever present neon beer signs and a banner promoting Beach House, there were no decorations. For all intents and purposes, the place was bare. With the windows clear, the place was also a lot brighter. He started to turn around when something else caught his eye. There was one window still covered in black and white paint. He cocked his head to the side for a different angle. There were straight lines. There were curved lines. Some crossed. Some did not. He sharpened his angle of vision.

Bobby's voice behind him caused his head to snap upright. "What're you looking at?" the bartender said.

Adam pointed toward the window in question. "That."

"You like that, huh?"

Adam dropped his arm. "I can't say I like it or dislike it. I never noticed it before."

"It's been there since Halloween," Bobby said.

"Halloween!"

"Yeah. You know Betty, the kitchen manager, she does all the window decorations for the various seasons... does a great job too. But I asked her keep that one up."

"Why?"

"I like it."

"What is it?" Adam asked.

"What does it look like to you?" Bobby countered.

"If I didn't know any better, I'd say it was an inkblot... you know, one of those things you use to try and figure out someone's personality. The last time I saw one of these was in medical school."

"Well, Adam, you do know better, because that's exactly what it is. Betty does one window like that every year."

"An inkblot? Why?

"You know, Halloween. Let's get scary... let's get into people's minds. It's always an interesting conversation piece, especially when people have had too much to drink."

"I bet." Adam turned and faced Bobby. "It's March. Halloween's been over for months."

"Yeah, but you're still here."

Adam squinted. "What's that mean?"

"Just what I said. You're still here. I look at you, I look at the inkblot there, and I see a lot of similarities."

This was one of those times when Adam knew he should be angry at Bobby for getting so personal. However, as in the past, his curiosity

170

overrode any feeling of anger. "I'm listening," he said.

Bobby looked around to make sure there were no prying ears nearby. "You're one of the most interesting inkblots I've ever met."

"Me! How's that?"

"What is an inkblot?" Bobby said. He pulled a *Doug* and didn't wait for an answer. "An inkblot is a design that can be interpreted in many different ways, depending on the person looking at it. Somebody explained it to me once as the 'glass half emptied half filled' question multiplied a hundred times over. There's no right or wrong answer, there's only a direction... a perception from which the inkblot is viewed. You... your life is an inkblot. A very interesting one I might add, but an inkblot nonetheless. Now, oftentimes there are certain parts of an inkblot that aren't all that difficult to figure out." He pointed to the window that initiated the discussion. "It doesn't take a rocket scientist to see that in the middle of Betty's design, there's a black cat with its tail straight up in the air."

Adam turned and looked at the window. He easily saw what Bobby was referring to. "Go on."

"There's no doubt you are one of the world's premier brain surgeons."

"Pediatric neurosurgeon," Adam corrected.

"Whatever," Bobby laughed. "That's who you are. But like the cat in the window, that's where the easiness ends. The rest of you–that's the mysterious part of the window–depending on how you look at it is what you see."

"What do you see?" Adam asked, his curiosity still high.

Bobby gave Adam one of those *do you really want me to* looks. Adam nodded and the bartender continued. "From my perspective, I see a brilliant brain surgeon... pediatric brain surgeon... who is wasting his life away down here instead of being out there in the real world boring holes or whatever it is you do into little people's skulls. What I see are people out there waiting for you... hoping... praying to God... that you will take their case and save their child's life. Or maybe it's a family who's hoping that you will come to their rescue and separate their two kids who, for some God forsaken reason, were born with their heads glued together. What I see is a man who has the talent... the hands, maybe not to save the world, but to at least save a few people in it, and then to teach others to do the same. What I see is a man who has been coming in here of late with a beautiful woman at his side who is about as perfect as one can get, only who can't seem to see just how lucky he is."

"From a different perspective... your perspective if I may... I see a self-absorbed genius, feeling totally sorry for himself... a pathetic human being wallowing in self-pity who can't seem to find his

172

way past the past. Yes, life dealt you a horrible hand... heavy bars for sure. I can't even begin to imagine. Yet, life also dealt you a set of hands that can do things no others can. Life also dealt you a second chance... a second chance with a woman who you seem to ignore for the most part. Why do you think she sits there and plays Buzztime all the time? Because she has nothing else to fill her own void. You know, you're not the only one to be fucked over in life. We all have bars of some sort to deal with. Yours are especially thick, I agree. But so are hers."

Bobby glanced away. "Her husband was one of my best friends. I was working that day she called and asked me to come over right away. I could tell by her voice something was wrong. I could feel in my heart just what it was, too. I prayed I was wrong, but when I saw the car sitting outside her house..." Bobby stopped and wiped his face with his sleeve. "That was a long time ago, and we've both moved on. We haven't forgotten him, nor has it been easy, but we've moved on. The bars are still there, but..." He looked over toward the ink-blot. "It's all a matter of which way you look at the window, pal." He turned and disappeared into the kitchen.

Adam spun and faced the window. He tipped his head to the side. At that moment, all he saw was a blur.

The next day

Adam watched the next few waves come up onto the beach to make sure he wasn't parked too close to the water. Satisfied, he leaned back and stared at the ocean. The sun was an hour off the horizon. The sky was clear. Seas were calm with gentle swells caressing the beach. Even with the lingering chill from the night before, the warmth of the sun was felt through the front windshield of the Jeep. He took a tentative sip of coffee. It wasn't too hot, so he took a bigger drink. The caffeine began to work its magic.

He didn't have all that much to drink the night before, but he still felt hung over. He tried rationalizing it–mixing B&B with V.O., too many nachos, too much noise. He knew that wasn't it. He felt bad because he hadn't slept well, and he hadn't slept well because his head was swirling with a tornado of thoughts, all surrounded by a black cat with its tail in the air. Bobby's words from the night before had been digging at his mind, and the cat's claws were only getting sharper. Adam tried to be angry as a way of minimizing their effect. He failed, instead feeling...

He paused in his thoughts. "Just how do you feel?" he said aloud.

A seagull landed in front of the Jeep. It looked at Adam, its head cocked to the side. "Get over it," the seagull seemed to say with a loud squawk.

"Easier said than done," Adam replied, as he watched the bird fly away. He watched a few more gulls fly over the water in their perpetual search for food. "Get over it," he repeated. "But how... how the fuck how?"

His hands on the steering wheel, he dropped his head into his arms. His eyes began to water. The normal human response was to wipe the tears away. His simply dropped onto his arms. There was no need to hide the tears. There was no need to hide his emotions. He didn't have to show strength to anyone. He was not leading a surgical team, talking to frightened parents, lecturing a group of frightened residents. He was doing none of that. He had none of that. He was alone in the world... alone in his misery... alone in his pain. Loneliness... the most dangerous emotion of all.

He looked up. Another seagull landed in front of the Jeep. Another squawk. Another message. He was alone in the world... alone in his misery... alone in his pain.

"Are you really alone?" the seagull asked.

St Patrick's Day 2009

Depending on your perspective, there are several times of the year to definitely be at Smitty

Behind Bars

McGee's (or to definitely stay away). These include the Fourth of July, New Year's Eve, the days of biker's week and Halloween. They tend to be the busiest and the most chaotic. However, none comes close to the spectacle of Smitty's on St. Patrick's Day. The line starts forming outside around 6:00 am. Shortly after the doors open at 10:30, the place is filled to capacity and stays that way until closing. It is the only time of the year beverages are served in plastic cups. And except perhaps for an indoor sports arena or a football stadium, it was the noisiest venue Adam had ever experienced.

This St. Patrick's Day started with an old fashioned Irish breakfast bar of corned beef and hash, eggs and green pancakes. Sunny brought a bag pipe band down from Philadelphia to play in the morning. Lunch started the $3.17 corned beef and cabbage special that ran the rest of the day. More live music followed. And the day went on. Night came, and the atmosphere never changed. If anything, it became even more frenzied. Every staff member was there at the opening. Everyone worked till closing and no one complained. It was their biggest payday of the year.

Mel warned Adam about all this ahead of time, but when he arrived shortly before twelve, he was still surprised to see the number of people milling about outside. While there was a 'no drinking in public' law in Delaware, so long as the booze

176

stayed away from the vehicles, the police did little to interfere with the party. Sunny and company patrolled the outside on a regular basis to ensure no one even close to the legal limit got behind the wheel.

Needless to say, it was also the local cab company's biggest day.

Mel came over during a break in her appointments and the two worked their way inside. Luckily, they found a couple of freshly vacated stools in the far corner. Doug saw them, and drinks were passed down like at a football stadium. A toast was made and they took their first drink of the day almost exactly at the stroke of noon.

Adam people watched and sipped his whisky. Mel did the same, sipping a water with lemon. People came by and spoke to Adam. He greeted them in return. They'd lean in closer to Mel to chit chat. Mel seemed to know everyone and everyone seemed to know her. She was friendly, yet she still seemed to keep her distance. People could get close, but not too close. It was like she was surrounded by a moat. He noticed this before but never gave it much thought until now when an older gentleman sporting a VFW cap stopped by, gave her a kiss on the cheek and a vigorous handshake. He then stepped back and snapped a smart salute. Suddenly, Adam realized that as a military widow, she was put on a pedestal above

Behind Bars

the other women in the bar.

Mel turned her back to the crowd to hide the tears welling up in her eyes. Adam crossed the moat as his arm encircled her waist and pulled her into him. She didn't resist as her head dropped to his shoulder. He put his mouth up to her ear and said, "I can't understand completely, but I can understand some." He gave her a tighter squeeze.

Wiping away the tears, she looked up at him. "Thank you," she said.

"What was your husband's name?"

She gave him a half-smile. "Richard... Richard O'Grady."

Adam's face paled. "Irish!"

"Definitely."

"I'm sorry."

"Don't be. This was his favorite day of the year. Claimed he liked it more than Christmas. He had two tattoos, one on each arm. My initials were on the left. The one on his right was a green shamrock."

Adam held up his cup. "Then here's to Richard O'Grady. May he be up there somewhere having a pint with us."

"I'm sure he is," Mel said. "I'm sure he is."

Adam took a long swallow of his drink. "What do you think your husband would be telling you on this day?"

"The same thing I imagine Nancy... that was

178

her name, right?"

Adam nodded.

"The same thing Nancy would be telling you. Get over it." Adam's complexion again paled. "Did I say something wrong?" Mel added.

"No, not at all," Adam chuckled. "It's just that's exactly what a seagull told me recently."

"A seagull?" Mel smiled. "Did the seagull tell you anything else?"

Adam stared her hard in the eyes. "No," he lied. "But if it did, it would have told me that the next time I had a beautiful woman in my arms, I should give her a kiss."

"And how would you have responded?"

"Smart bird."

Mel started to laugh, only to have her reaction cut off by Adam's lips contacting hers. Almost as if embarrassed by what he had done, Adam started to pull away. She, however, reached up and wrapped her arm around his neck. She had waited a long time for this moment, not only the months since she had met Adam, but years since... years since the unmarked car pulled into her driveway.

She held on for as long as she dared before releasing her grip. Their lips parted. She smiled. "So you can speak to seagulls, huh?"

"Evidently, I can."

"Well, the next time you see that seagull, tell him I said thanks."

Adam smiled. "I'll do that." He was about to kiss her again when there was a tap on his shoulder. Two plates of corned beef and cabbage were being passed their way. He looked up to find Bobby burying them in his smile. Adam nodded and returned the sentiment. He wondered if Bobby had seen what had just happened. Probably, he thought. Not much got past that bartender.

Adam and Mel ate their corned beef and cabbage in silence. They looked at each other once in a while. Body parts touched. Smiles were exchanged. In all the chaos surrounding them, Adam felt at peace for the first time in many months. With a mouthful of cabbage, he leaned over and gave Mel a wet kiss in the cheek.

For her part, Mel made a mental note to go out to the beach in the next couple of days and thank the seagulls herself. She wondered if they were Irish.

*****

It wasn't all that busy a night. The band was on a break at the moment. People were talking. Drinks were refilled. Food orders were punched into the computer. And rock music blared from the ceiling speakers. The numbers didn't match St. Patty's Day the week before, but it was still a lively crowd–more people were standing than sitting. A few were even dancing to the music playing.

Adam took a sip of his drink, the third of the night. He wondered on more than one occasion what the place would be like if there was actually a dance floor. He had mentioned that to Bobby just the night before who told him that Sunny had considered that in the past, but decided against it. Besides taking up space, it would take away from the intimacy of the environment. People liked being close to the band. "So close," Adam had responded, "that they're right in each other's faces?"

To which Bobby replied, "Exactly. People like to connect with the musicians, and vice versa. It gives the performance a more personal touch and makes people feel special–and people like to feel special."

"They also don't like to feel lonely," Adam said to himself.

He took a sip of his drink and glanced down the bar where Bobby stood talking to Sunny. It was obvious the owner was irritated about something, and the bartender was getting the brunt of the attack. Being the man he was, Bobby just stood there and nodded as if agreeing with everything the owner was saying–which was the right thing to do considering Sunny was not only the owner, she was a woman; and from what Adam had seen so far, a very strong willed woman at that. *Yes, ma'am* was definitely in order.

The conversation lasted another thirty seconds and then Sunny turned and stormed into the kitchen. Her short stature made the effect of the storm even more intense. Bobby eventually made his way down to Adam after first replenishing drinks along the way. Flattening both hands down on the bar, he said, "fuckin' bastard." Before Adam could ask for an explanation, the bartender continued. "I went out on a limb for that boy. He'd been out of school a couple years and was trying to get money together to go to college. He was accepted at Salisbury, but couldn't afford it. So he came to me and I went to Sunny and asked her for a favor. And what's he go and do? Fucks me over."

Adam remained silent a moment and let some of the steam clear the area. After a sip of his drink, he said, "who's he?"

"David... you know, the tall thin bar-back. He's been with us for over a year, and was actually doing quite well. He didn't know squat about the business when he first came here. Again, I had to talk Sunny into hiring him as we usually don't hire green backs. Anyway, he was doing fine, making good money and going to school, just like he wanted. He was even talking about becoming a bartender when he found out he could make more money tending bar than he could as a teacher." Bobby shook his head in disgust. "Anyway, this is the second day in a row he hasn't shown up for work... hasn't called either." Bobby pulled in a deep breath and looked away a moment. Adam could tell there was both anger and hurt in his eyes. Another breath and the bartender continued. "Sunny called his apartment and one of his roommates answered and said he was at work. She asked where he was working, and they said he had just started a new job at Nathan's... that's a new place that just opened up on 78th Street. Supposed to be really swanky and all that. But... the owner, a guy named Nathan Roberts, is a real sleaze ball. This'll be the third or fourth place he's opened down here, and all have failed."

"Why?" Adam asked instinctively.

"He talks a good story, gets people to back him financially and others to come work for him. Then he screws them. He doesn't know diddly shit about running a restaurant or a bar."

"Then why's he do it?"

"Don't kid yourself. He makes his money out of the project. When he figures he can't soak any more out of the sponge, he just shuts the place down. Story goes the last time he didn't even give his people warning. They showed up to work one day and the doors were locked. Naturally, it was pay week."

"Anyway, he comes in here once in a while... nosing around and asking a lot of questions. I guess he's trying to learn how to run a business the right way. He was in here the other day. I guess he got his claws into David... made him a lot of promises and stuff like that."

"Why do you let him come in here?" Adam said somewhat surprised.

Bobby laughed. "He's a scum bag, but he tips well. Besides, if you're going to bar somebody from coming into your establishment, you'd better have a good reason. Being a scum bag isn't one of them. All he would need is a reason to sue our ass, and we'd be in deep shit. Even though you usually win these kind of things, the cost for lawyers is high."

"He has a cost, too," Adam pointed out.

Bobby laughed. "He is a lawyer."

"Why wouldn't David tell you he was leaving?" Adam asked.

Bobby shrugged his shoulders. "Probably too embarrassed. Roberts probably told him not to say anything anyway."

"Well, maybe he will make out better there," Adam said as a way of support.

"Probably will... the first few months. Then when the going gets tough..."

"He can always go somewhere else."

"Not in this town," Bobby said. "He'll be black-balled. You expect a high turnover in this business, and you get it. But there's a level of integrity that goes along with it."

"He's young," Adam argued.

184

"Bullshit. He's in college. If he's smart enough to do that, he's smart enough to know how to treat his employer."

Adam stared at the bartender and said, "let me give *you* a friendly piece of advice. Never ever associate intelligence with common sense. The stories I could tell you about some of the most brilliant doctors I know who do the stupidest things."

"Your point?"

Adam smiled. "Don't write the boy off just yet."

Bobby smiled back. "You don't understand, Adam. In the ballgame at Smitty McGee's, you only get two strikes and then you're out."

"Fair enough," Adam conceded. "But he's only had one swing."

Bobby shrugged his shoulders. "This is a tough business."

"Show me one that isn't," Adam challenged. "Good employees, even those who are rough around the edges, are hard to come by."

Bobby shrugged again. "You just don't see the ethics in the work place with these young people. Hell, if we had been busy tonight, Sunny would have really been on a rampage."

Adam chuckled. "Just remember what an old chief resident told me once, sticks and stones can break your bones, but only words can fire you. So if she didn't fire you, you're okay."

"Whatever."

*****

Bobby looked over at the corner of the bar where Max, Beach House's harmonica player, was putting romance in the air. Shaking his head side to side, the bartender said, "you know Adam, I can figure most things out in this place, but that's one I ain't got yet."

"What's that?" Adam said, turning in the same direction. The place was crowded and noisy enough there was no need to worry about staring, not that anyone seemed to worry about that in the first place.

Bobby continued. "He's in his sixties, nice, but not all that good looking; and he adds more love to this place than anybody. It's only a harmonica for God's sakes. How does he do it?"

Adam contemplated the question before responding. "He's good with his lips."

Bobby stared at the doctor and broke into his wide smile. "You know, Adam, you're okay. There's…"

Adam's hand snapped up in the air. "Don't say it!"

Bobby smiled and gave his customer a wink.

And then he was gone.

But not before the thought was imprinted in Adam's mind. Was there… was there hope for him? A few months ago, he wouldn't have even contemplated the question. Now, however...

Adam redirected his attention back to the harmonica player. The man was good... very good. And he claimed he couldn't read music. "What am I good at?" Adam mouthed. His eyes went down to his hands, which slowly encircled his glass of whisky.

The next musical selection featured Sparks the bass player and Sal in a prolonged instrumental improvisation. It was something they did time to time–usually spur of the moment. Ricky blended into the melody as his lead and bass guitarist spoke to one another through music. Sal contorted his face with each passing riff and was rewarded with Spark's smile of validation. Ricky looked on, keeping in rhythm with the duo and obviously in awe as the two guitarists played like classical virtuosos, only Smitty McGee's style. The beer and bourbon gave the action juice.

The crowd loved it. It was pure entertainment, medicine for the soul. It eased away the aches and pains of living. It was the kind of entertainment places like Smitty's offered as a buffer zone to help their patrons put away the tears and bring on the cheers. It served another purpose for couples in love, or headed that way. It was the artist's canvas for what was to come.

After a rousing applause, Ricky took the band into a slow piece. One loving couple danced, oblivious to everything except each other. "Lay your head upon my shoulder," Ricky sang smoothly. "Move your warm and tender body close to mine."

Before Adam could fully digest the lyrics, Mel's head was on his shoulder and she whispered in his ear, "you feel good next to me."

"The feeling's mutual," he said. To himself, he added, "maybe I am good at something."

April 2009

Bobby and Doug were close enough to where Adam could hear their conversation without effort. A couple key words caused him to actually focus on their words. Shoes and watches–not what one would expect bartenders to be discussing during a momentary lull in the action. Doug saw Adam looking their way and stepped over. Bobby followed. "How many watches do you own, Adam?" Doug asked.

It took Adam a second to come up with the answer. "Two," he said.

"Two!" Doug exclaimed. "Only two?"

"Yeah, but they're probably both Rolexes," Bobby said.

Again, Adam hesitated. "Actually, I don't own a Rolex. Mine are both cheapos." He held his left wrist out that sported a silver faced watch with a heavy silver band. "I bought this one from my jeweler on 5th Avenue in New York, right outside Tiffany's."

"Right outside... as if on the street?" Doug said.

"Yeah, twenty bucks and I've had it for over five years... good deal, huh?"

Doug shrugged his shoulders. "How about shoes? How many pairs of shoes do you own?"

More hesitation on Adam's part. "Three... no four. I have a pair of winter boots."

"Only four," Doug said. Being the taller of the two bartenders, he leaned over and looked down towards Adam's feet. "Boat shoes, huh?"

Adam glanced down as well. "Yeah, that's pretty much all I wear."

Doug straightened up. "What a deprived man. What a deprived man. Only two watches and four pairs of shoes!"

Adam sat quietly, unsure whether he should feel insulted or not. Doug had a way of doing that to you, saying something you weren't really sure which way to take. Finally, "what's so important about watches and shoes?"

"What's so important about watches and shoes?" Doug bellowed. "They make the man, Adam. They make the man. You see, women, they expect a man to be clean and to dress nicely. The adage that clothes make the man is true. But what sets one man apart from the other are the accessories. And by accessories I don't mean heavy chains dangling around your neck, or flashy rings on your fingers. I'm talking about things a little more subtle, like watches and shoes. That's where it's at. For you to buy an expensive shirt and an expensive pair of pants, and then show up at her front door in boat shoes... well, that's a bit much." He turned and glanced at his coworker. "Don't you think, Bobby?"

"Most definitely," Bobby agreed. "Why, at last count, Doug here has over a hundred pairs of shoes and over twenty watches, and none of them bought off the street either."

"Bobby isn't far behind," Doug piped in. Seeing a customer settle up to the bar, Doug moved in that direction.

"Go figure," Adam said, genuinely surprised at what he had just heard.

Bobby leaned forward. "But you've got to be careful with all that, too."
"How so?

"Now I don't have anything against them, but you don't want women to think, you know, you're gay."

Adam laughed. "I don't think you have to worry about that."

"You never know," Bobby said.

Adam continued to laugh. "So what do you do about that?"

Bobby straightened up and flashed one of his smiles. "I make sure I own more guns than shoes."

190

*****

Bobby and Adam had been talking about nothing in particular–a common occurrence at the bar–when somehow or other the conversation got around to the relationship between staff and customers. The conversation was basically one-sided–also a common occurrence. "The last thing we want to do when our shift is over is come over on that side and sit with you all," Bobby lamented. "Yet, you all think it's cool to sit with us and buy us drinks." Bobby motioned to his left where Sunny was surrounded by a trio of golfers. "Take those three guys over there. It was like Sunny was their American Idol... which is probably true, at least right now. It's the same thing when Ricky and the other members of the band take a break and mingle with the crowd. People have always wanted to rub shoulders with those they consider celebrities–and yes, bartenders sometimes fall into that category.

Adam laughed. "If you don't like it, why do it?"

Bobby chuckled as well. "Finances, man. Finances." He went on to explain without being coached. "We drink for free. All we do is tip one another. But when you buy me a drink, that goes on your tab."

"What about Sunny over there?" Adam said, nodding in that direction.

Bobby explained. "Number one, she's just a friendly outgoing person. Secondly, she doesn't participate in the ritual, arguing that she's working, but I've seen Doug pour two rounds of shots since you and I've been talking. Now, she'll probably set up the third round on her, but that will probably lead to a fourth. On top of that, like I said, Sunny's a celebrity in her own right."

"So, it is all about the money?" Adam said.

"Much of life is a big hustle," Bobby replied. He held his hand up in anticipation of a rebuke. "Don't tell me medicine isn't the same way. Now you may travel overseas to some undeveloped country to dig out a brain tumor from some poor kid, and you may do it for free, but when you come back to the states and operate at your own hospital, you don't work there for free. And what do you get when, let's say, you go to some big ass conference in London and talk about what you did for that child in Africa? I suspect the lecture fees makes up for the pro bono work." He nodded his head towards Sunny. "The pro bono shots are the same." He paused. "Yes, Adam, life's a big fuckin' hustle."

Adam smiled. "Well then Bobby my friend, next time you sit with me, you buy your own drinks."

Bobby broke into a smile and said, "There are exceptions to every rule." He turned and headed toward another group of patrons who had just come through the door.

*****

"Did you ever notice," Bobby said stopping by with a couple of shots. "There's always some old guy at the bar who thinks he can't dance and really can, and there's always some drunk chick who thinks she can dance and can't? Then, there's always someone with big boobs who you wish would."

*****

Doug, in his normal *anything goes at a bar* attitude, was conversing with a couple ladies one evening. As usual, not only was the conversation of the anything goes variety, it was also loud and available for anyone to eavesdrop without effort. The discussion centered on the virtues of dating around versus being in a steady relationship. One of the ladies was arguing her side of the coin, which was on the side of a steady relationship. Doug, to no one's surprise, debated the opposite. He was especially going at the advantage of having a variety of partners, arguing that variety kept things fresh. The lady countered that was a lame excuse for being lazy. She said that even in a steady relationship you should be able to keep things fresh if you put some time and effort into it.

The debate continued with one lady talking, the other sitting quietly and sipping her beer. Finally, Doug looked her way and said, "you've been listening to all this. What do you think?"

The non-debating lady set her beer down and said, "It doesn't matter what I say, Doug. Your opinion will always be your opinion. Matter of fact, you're one of the most opinionated people I've ever met. You've got a heart of gold, Doug. Many people can't see that, but I do. You'd give a dead dog in the middle of the road the shirt off your back if you thought it'd do any good. But to get to that heart of gold, a person has to go through a lot of shit. Quite frankly, I don't feel like doing that tonight, so it doesn't matter what I think."

Now there wasn't much that got Doug the pontificator tongue tied, but she managed to do so. "Let me ask you this, then," Doug said in a recovery mode. "Are you sexually active?"

During this time, the surrounding patrons were all looking elsewhere, even though their ears were all tuned into WDOUG on their FM dials. With the last question, however, all eyes found the speakers. Without batting an eye and without much hesitation, she said, "no, Doug, I'm not active. I just lie there when I have sex... like a dead dog in the middle of the road."

It had been a long time since Adam heard Smitty McGee's so silent. It had been a long time since

Adam had seen so many mouths drop open in unison. It had been a long time since Adam had seen Doug speechless twice in such a short a period of time. Doug's mouth was open, but the well of orations was dry. In the WDOUG radio world, there were few times in life when silence was golden. This was one of them now. And much to the bartender's credit, he acknowledged the moment. Without any further ado, he simply turned and walked away, ignoring the applause and whistles behind him.

*****

Advice from your friendly bartender: Don't fuck with the people who handle your food.

*****

Last call was an interesting time at a bar. There was usually a rush of people who came in wanting to get a quick buzz on before going home. There were also those who ordered food for carry out. Adam watched in amazement at how many people were out and about at this hour of the night, and this was only one bar. Who were they? What were their stories? He could understand if it was an occasional occurrence, but from what he saw, it was a nightly ritual. Bobby claimed that during the off season, the last forty-five minutes could account for fifty percent of the entire evening. He also said that because many of the late arrivals worked in the food and beverage industry, the tips were extra fine. Bobby called it the storm before the calm.

It was something Adam found himself experiencing more and more of late. "Was that good or bad?" he wondered, as his glass was filled for the final time of the evening.

15

Mid April 2009

Definition of a hangover: three hours of pleasure, six hours of sleep, and then fourteen hours of hell.

*****

Overheard at the bar one evening: "I can't believe the crazy things people do these days. Why, I was sitting in church last Sunday when this woman next to me lit up a cigarette. How rude, I thought. Why, I almost dropped my beer."

*****

Because it was Wednesday and bikers' night, Adam sat around the far corner near the entrance of the kitchen. Not that he had anything against the bikers in that he had been here for several Wednesdays now and had come to enjoy the experience; he just didn't want to mingle with them and get in their way. Into his second drink, he happened to look down and notice there was a small gold plaque beneath his cocktail napkin. The metal was worn so he couldn't read the inscription. He looked to his right and saw a couple more such plaques, again unreadable because of wear. When Bobby did a fly-by with a drink refill, Adam asked about the plaques.

Bobby set his drink down, reached over and polished the smudge marks off the one directly to Adam's right. "These are in memorial to people who used to sit there. In your case, it was old man Jack, and that's what he drank, too–straight up, no ice. He'd come in several times a week, usually after he got off work–never knew what he actually did, though it was rumored he owned several apartment buildings in town. So he was probably rich as a bitch. Anyway, he'd come in and walk over to his spot. If it was empty, he sat down. If it was occupied, and the person saw and knew him, the stool was vacated. If it was a stranger though, and they didn't get the message they were sitting in somebody's seat, old man Jack would never say a word. He'd just simply leave."

"He wouldn't sit anywhere else?" Adam said.

"Never saw him sit anywhere else as long as I worked here," Bobby said.

"Why the plaque then?"

"He's dead," Bobby said solemnly.

"Dead!" Adam looked downward. A chill went up his spine. Sliding off the seat, he decided to go mingle with the biker crowd.

*****

The song started with a few strums of the guitar and Ricky singing into the mike. He wasn't enunciating words. He was just making sounds. A few bars later, Max stepped up to the mike and started mimicking him with the harmonica. The song was fun, and quite creative as the two sounds meshed. Ricky would sing a few bars. Max would copy them. Then Max would lead. The piece went on for several minutes, with the crowd getting more and more into the song as it continued. Finally with a flourish, it ended and the crowd erupted in cheers and applause.

Adam, who had been listening with great curiosity, turned to Mel and said, "I've heard them do that before. I guess it doesn't have a name."

"Matter of fact, it does," Mel replied. "It's called *The Daba Daba Blaba Blaba Dinga Dinga Ding Dong Blues*."

"You're kidding?"

"There's no way I could have just made that up."

Adam shrugged his shoulders and laughed. "You never know what you're going to hear or see here, do you?"

"That's why it's called a raw bar," Mel said. "It's unrehearsed."

As Mel went back to her game, Adam pulled a cocktail napkin from the pile and a pen from his pocket. With a smile on his face, he started writing. "It's unrehearsed..." The smile faded as he added, "just like life."

*****

Travis was tall. He was quiet. He tended to stay in the background even during breaks. He definitely didn't have the muscles of someone like Bon Jovi's drummer, but man, could he play. It wasn't often in such a band that the drummer did anything other than keep the beat, but tonight was different. Tonight, for whatever reason, he was being showcased. And the crowd loved it. It had been many years since Adam heard *Wipeout*. He didn't recall ever hearing it live. But he was tonight. Big muscles or not, Travis was on the mark. When the piece was finished, there was the biggest applause Adam had heard at Smitty McGee's. Travis smiled meekly and evolved back to his usual subdued self. He twirled his sticks, nodded appreciation and started tapping out the rhythm for the next song.

*****

Ricky sang a Joe Brooks song:

You light up my life.
You give me hope,
To carry on.
You light up my days,
And fill my nights with song.

Adam listened to a few more bars, and then looked over at Mel, who was playing trivia. While concentrating intensely, she still wore a soft smile. Adam decided to wear one too.

It was a lively crowd. Booze and food flowed freely across the bar. The shot monkey was especially busy, including frequent hand offs to the band. At the midnight hour when the entertainment was scheduled to stop, the crowd was just starting to peak. Beers were refilled and additional shots poured. The band played another thirty minutes while the crowd danced, cheered and enjoyed the music. When they finally called it a night, the group broke down their equipment with the help of a few in the crowd. The staggering of feet was evident. There was an occasional need to grab a wall as the floor failed to hold still beneath them.

"Who's driving them home tonight?" Adam

asked Bobby on one of his fly-bys.

Bobby looked at the band. "They'll be okay."

"Okay? They can't even stand up straight."

"God will look after them."

"God? What about the police?"

"Oh, they'll look after them, too." Bobby motioned with his head to the opposite end of the bar. "Eddie and Alex down there are off duty Fenwick Island cops. One'll drive the van. The other will follow."

"Sunny set that up?"

"Yeah, she gives them a call when it looks like they're going to be too wasted to get home on their own. If Eddie or Alex can't make it, someone else will show up."

"Smart call," Adam acknowledged.

"Sunny's a smart woman," Bobby said.

As if on cue, Sunny came around the corner and headed toward Bobby and Adam. It was obvious she had her eyes on Bobby with something important on her mind.

"Uh, oh," Bobby said. "Something's got her goat."

Before Adam could reply, she was at Bobby's side. "Hi," she hissed.

Not known for mincing words, Bobby replied, "what's got your goat?"

"What makes you think something has my goat?"

"Intuition."

She started to object, but said instead, "next person calls out sick around here is toast. Is that understood?"

"Toast, as in something you put jam and butter on?" Bobby queried.

"Toast as in fired," Sunny snapped.

Bobby looked over at Adam and gave him an *I told you so* shrug of the shoulders.

"The next person..." Adam injected. "Does that mean customers, too?" He followed his comment with a wide smile.

"Damn right it does," Sunny said. She turned and started back toward her office. She stopped, however, after a couple steps and turned around. She stared at the duo. "You know, Adam, I don't know what you do, but you've got a good head on your shoulders. You ever want a job, just let me know."

Bobby broke into laughter and started to speak. Before he could say anything, Adam reached across the bar and grabbed his arm. "You're toast if you say a word," Adam threatened. Bobby continued laughing and waved Sunny back to her office.

"You're a smart man," Adam said.

"At one time in your life, you were, too," Bobby said. He turned and walked away.

Adam turned and looked at Mel, who had taken in the conversation without uttering a word. She leaned toward him and put her arm through his.

Behind Bars

"Being smart is like riding a bicycle," she said. "You never forget how to do it. When you fall off, you just have to have the courage to get back on. But don't worry, that'll come with time."

Adam tilted his head to the side as the earlier song came to mind. "You give me hope..."

*****

Adam watched as three women paid their bill, flirted with Bobby for the final time and slid off their respective bar stools. There was some staggering as each regained her balance. There were embarrassing smiles, followed by giggles, followed by promises that each was okay. Holding onto each other, they headed for the door.

As Bobby headed toward the cash register with their payment in hand, Adam said, "I have but one question to ask about those three."

"What's that?" Bobby said, stopping to refill Adam's glass.

"Who's driving?"

Bobby laughed. "Beats me, but that'll be a chapter in our book." He reached into a cup sitting beside the cash register and pulled out a set of keys. "Oops," he said, dangling them in the air.

*****

While trying to be subtle, the conversation was actually becoming quite loud and lively. Bobby was leaning over the bar talking to one of the regulars, who as usual, was drunk and having a good time. For whatever reason, she had set her sights on Bobby for the night. She was tall, thin and well built. Adam surmised correctly that much of her body was of the industrialized variety. Bobby had commented in that past he would like to take her to a dark room, but he always added that would never happen.

At this particular moment, he was explaining why to her, "I will break almost any rule known to mankind, but there are a few I will not do battle with," he said. "For one, I will not fuck thy neighbor's wife. I've told you that before."

The man sitting beside Adam spouted out, "hey Bobby, if you don't want her, I'll take her."

As he turned and walked away, the bartender put his left hand behind him and flashed the man the bird.

There was a good round of laughter. Then one of locals sitting near Adam pointed to the corner of the bar where a young man who barely looked legal had one arm wrapped around a bottle of beer, the other around the waist of a blonde. "Our boy there's slipping," the local said.

"How's that?" another local sitting beside him inquired.

"He's been with the same girl three weeks in a

row. He's usually with a new one every week."

"You sure?"

"I'm sure."

"Damn, must be serious," the drinking partner said.

"Or no other alternative," the first man said.

"There's always an alternative." The two men laughed.

Adam started to laugh with them but cut the sound short. There was something about the conversation... something one of them said... something that struck a nerve.

And it had nothing to do with Bobby flashing them the bird or the young man having his arm around a beautiful girl.

*****

Adam sat on the back deck and stared into the darkness. He did that a lot lately when he got home from the bar. It was a quiet contemplation, a hiatus from the high level of stimulation he left behind. It was good to take a breath of fresh air, to relax, to let his senses cool down, to return to his cave, to return to his hibernation. It gave him a chance to mull over the evening.

The night felt short. He arrived late and left soon after the band finished at midnight. Bobby was training a new bartender. He was attentive and friendly, yet he just didn't have the swagger of Bobby.

Then again, no one had the swagger of Bobby. No wonder the cougars saw him as a delicacy. "Who needs sushi when we have Bobby?" a woman said one evening.

Adam had said little. He simply watched the crowd while Mel played Buzztime. He listened specifically to the conversation between the two regulars sitting nearby. The two men had talked about a lot of things that evening. They each had children, so one was griping about the cost of college tuition, the other about the cost of shoes. They talked about golf, how they played earlier that day and where they were going to play next. There were the comments about the young man having the same girl three weeks in a row. That's where Adam's mind got stuck. Something one of them said held the rest of Adam's thoughts hostage.

He pulled his attention away from the two men, thinking instead about whether he needed to turn on the AC, or he could... His train of thought derailed. He stared out into the darkness.

Or as an alternative, he could open a window.

The one man said, "there's always an alternative."

While the concept certainly wasn't a new revelation, it did cause Adam to pause. He had survived these many months by keeping his life simple, his thinking superficial–even as he grew friendlier with Bobby, Mel and the others at Smitty's. And even after he told his story on New Year's, he returned to the cave. Some might call it a defense mechanism. Others might label the behavior as survival instincts. After all, most creatures in the animal kingdom survived by living very simple lives.

To Adam, however, it didn't matter. He lived that way because he saw no...

"There's always an alternative," he said aloud.

16

Early May 2009

The Harborside Bar and Grill was crowded. All stools around the bar were filled. The tables outside on the covered deck were the same. Those finishing a late lunch were rapidly replaced by others anxious to get the afternoon happy hour started. The two female bartenders had not stopped hustling since Mel and Adam arrived an hour earlier. The bar-back, a tall, thin, curly haired man in his early thirties, weaved in and out of the two bartenders. Adam smiled as he watched the action. Same ballet, different stage.

Harborside was the home of the original orange crush, a drink consisting of freshly squeezed orange juice mixed with several different liquors. It was by far the most popular drink being served. Adam was still working on his first. Mel was working on her second. They sat together at the side bar, their backs toward the water. They sat close together as even the side bar was crowded. A three piece band played mostly covers in the corner. Mel leaned over and told Adam that the lead guitarist was one of the best in the area. Adam agreed. It was an older crowd, consisting mainly of locals from West Ocean City. Still, it was fun. The sport of people watching was the same regardless of where you went.

Besides having a taste for an orange crush, Mel wanted to come to Harborside to hear the band. She called it *chasing the music*. It was something she and her husband used to do when he was home. They made it a point every Saturday to go someplace different to hear a different band. It was one of the many things she missed in her life.

As they listened, sipped their drinks and munched on the complimentary peanuts, Mel talked to the people around her. Even though Mel had never met them before, it was like they were old friends. They talked about the weather, the local elections that were coming up in the fall and the weather some more. It seemed to Adam that no matter what you talked about or with whom, the conversation always contained at least a few sentences regarding Mother Nature. The reasoning was simple. While the weather had little, if any impact on his ability to earn a living; at the beach, the weather was everything. The weather could make you; the weather could break you... at any given hour... on any given day.

The hairdressing business was not immune.

Feeling the breeze pick up behind him, Adam spun around and stared across the water. It was a warm spring day. The humidity was high. Ominous clouds in the distance threatened to take the humidity higher. The forecast called for a chance of showers in the afternoon. A glance at the sky told even the most amateur meteorologist the word chance was an unnecessary addition to the forecast. He wondered about the impact of a thunderstorm on the local economy on this particular day. While it might have an impact someplace, it certainly wouldn't at the Harborside Bar and Grill. The place was already packed. He looked down at the boats tied alongside the restaurant's pier. They were mostly in the twenty to twenty-five foot range. All were open cockpit, and all were rigged for fishing. There was no such thing as a pure pleasure boat down here. The primary function of any watercraft (jets skis and pontoon boats excluded) was fishing. An auxiliary purpose of the boat was to ferry its owner and guests to local restaurants.

In contrast to these boats, an old work barge sat off east of the pier. The barge was empty except for an old rusting backhoe that sat in the middle. It was tied to the deck with chains. The deck was littered with broken shells where seagulls had dropped the oysters and clams from up high to break them open for ingestion. While the barge itself looked as if it had received little maintenance over the years, the dock lines were new, the excess coiled neatly by their respective cleats.

"If I were a photographer," Adam thought.

A seagull stood perched atop one of the heavy metal cleats on the waterside of the craft, its head jerking side to side. Waiting for what? Adam wasn't sure–until someone threw a peanut onto the barge.

Adam's gaze drifted across the narrow creek where another fleet of fishing boats was moored. Only unlike the small pleasure boats below him, these were massive mounds of rusting steel, outriggers and lines. This was the home of Ocean City's commercial fishing fleet. Adam smiled as he wondered how anyone in the world would know how to untangle the mumbo-jumbo mess of cables and lines that were intertwined amongst the outriggers and superstructures of the vessels. He had no doubt the puzzle was doable, and not nearly as complicated as it appeared to the untrained eye. Old and weathered, the vessels still looked powerful. The boats below him swayed as the unseen current flowed through the narrow waterway. The commercial fishing fleet just sat there, motionless, looming above the dilapidated bulkheads against which they were moored.

Adam's gaze moved further into the distance. A half a mile away he could see the tops of yet another set of boats. This was the charter fleet–the heart and soul of Ocean City fishing. Like soldiers in line for battle, they stood tall, their outriggers reaching high into the heavens. Blue fish, tuna, shark, blue marlin, and the symbol of Ocean City fishing, the white marlin–these were the deer of the sea these hundred thousand dollar plus yachts sought to capture. Someone once mentioned to Adam that these were awfully expensive deer stands. He didn't understand at the time. He did now as the fleet sat idle in the basin, waiting for either the world to win the lottery or the price of fuel to drop. Adam scanned the scene before him again. Small private fishing boats, an old rusting barge, the commercial fishing fleet, the charter fleet off in the distance–a contrast of images, all encased by and dependent upon the weather.

Adam refocused on the work barge where the seagull sat patiently waiting for someone else to throw him a peanut. But no one did. Its head cocked to the side, the bird squawked in protest.

Adam laughed as he muttered under his breath, "Get over it."

The light started to fade as the storm clouds rolled in from the west. A gust of wind blew through the bar and any paper products not anchored down with a drink blew away. Clear vinyl curtains were lowered and the scene now had a kaleidoscopic appearance to it. Adam watched as the rain worked its way across the water. As the first gust struck the metal roof over the bar, he turned around. There were glances upward, with everyone wondering the same thing. The worry was short lived. There was a drip here and a drip there, but overall the roof did its job. Adam turned his attention to Mel who had put her arm around his shoulder. One hand gently messaged the muscles of his back. The other was holding a bowl.

"Want a peanut?" she asked.

*****

Two days later, Bobby plopped down on the edge of the beer cooler and grabbed a couple of cheese fries sitting in front of Adam. Stuffing the food in his mouth, he said, "The cash register totals say we haven't been all that busy. My poor feet are certainly saying otherwise. I think this is the first time I've sat down since I got here." Adjusting his position, he looked around to make sure there were no empty glasses or bottles littering the bar. Happy hour was ending. Those who had been in for the discounted wings and oysters, and dollar drafts were finishing up. In another fifteen or twenty minutes, the entire bar would turn over– that is except for the regulars who'd hang around a little longer, have a couple of extra drinks and maybe something more substantial for dinner. Ever since he started bartending, Bobby always thought happy hour an interesting phenomenon.

It was certainly big business, and one of the most competitive times for bars. Sunny claimed that whoever won happy hour won the rest of the night. Bobby wasn't sure he understood the reasoning behind this, but if nothing else, happy hour kept the bar stools occupied during what would otherwise be a slow period of the day.

Bobby brought his focus back to the customer in front of him. "Anyway, what brings you out this time of the day?"

Adam wiped his mouth. "Cheap beer."

Bobby chuckled. "Nice try."

Adam shrugged his shoulders. "I guess I was out for a walk and this was the way the wind was blowing."

"A little better," Bobby jested. "Anyway, how you doing with our book?"

"Our book?"

"Yeah, our book."

Adam chuckled. "I imagine I've written about as many pages as you."

"Oh," Bobby said. "I guess that sort of puts us behind schedule, doesn't it?"

Adam laughed. "For something to be on schedule, it has to start."

Bobby reached up and tapped the side of his head. "It's started. I have everything right up here. I just have to find time to get it down on paper, that's all."

"That's all!" Adam exclaimed. "For your information, getting it down on paper is a big part of the project. Remember, people read the printed word, not minds."

"Well, I've given you some stuff," Bobby reminded.

Adam laughed.

Bobby laughed along with him. "Here's some more. How about 127½ feet?"

"Huh?"

"That's how long the bar is in here... the longest in the area. We officially seat a total of 274. We have ten beers on tap, another thirty some variety in bottles, and almost any kind of liquor you could want. There isn't a drink one of us can't make." The bartender turned his gaze upward. "There are a total of fifty TV screens. If there's a sports network available, we subscribe to it... Let me see... Oh yeah, we're open 364 days a year and have been here since 1989." Bobby looked at Adam with a big smile. "How's that for a start?"

"Sounds like an advertisement to me," Adam said. "But it is a start.

"If nothing else, it'll be fun," Bobby insisted.

"Writing is not fun. It's work," Adam said.

The writer-wanna-be leaned in and stared the doctor in the eye. "Then you're not writing about the right stuff." He stared at the doctor another moment before swaggering off toward a pair of ladies whose glasses were nearing empty.

He returned a few minutes later. "I'll give you one for the book," he said, setting an overfilled glass in front of Adam. "Do you know what it means when someone orders a strange drink such as half scotch and half cream?"

Adam nodded negatively.

"It means he's a complete alcoholic with stomach ulcers, and needs the cream to help handle the alcohol."

"Are people that desperate to drink?" Adam asked.

Bobby chuckled. "You have no clue."

He scanned the bar quickly. "Here's a couple more book items. The term *check the hood* means that someone in the kitchen has a fresh bowl packed. When you smoke it, you blow it out the hood vents so no one smells the dope. On the other hand, *in the weeds* means you're very busy."

"Too busy to go under the hood?" Adam said.

Bobby laughed again. "You're never too busy to go under the hood." He turned and headed toward another empty glass.

17

Mid May 2009

Carol Johnston threw her keys on her desk and took off her coat, hanging it on the back of the door like she did every day. She took down a brown sweater and put it on. Mrs. Rogers, several of the other people in the department teased. She didn't care though. Her office was an ice box, even in the summer. She paused as her hand went up to the white lab coat hanging on the same hook. It was freshly cleaned, waiting for its owner to return.

She pulled off a speck of lint and did an about face. She had too much to do today to let her mind go there. Besides, Adam had responded to her last email, saying he was okay, and adding that he was enjoying his daily walks. It was the first time he had mentioned anything other than he was alive. She told herself not to read more into the message. Still, it was a glimmer of hope.

She turned on the computer and waited for it to boot up. The first thing on the agenda was to check her email. She deleted the junk mail and responded to the rest where appropriate. For those inquiring about Dr. Singer, she gave her canned reply that he was doing well, thank you—the same canned message she received from him. If it was a close friend or colleague, she added that his spirits seemed more upbeat of late. There was nothing wrong, she told herself, with spreading around a little hope.

She had three more emails to go when her rapid fire routine came to a sudden halt. She opened up what was actually an email to Dr. Daniel Fitzgerald, the assistant chairman of the department, from the hospital president. Daniel had copied the email to her. There was nothing else. There was no direction as to what she should do. Then again, she really wouldn't expect anything else. The copied letter would be enough. Half-way through the letter, the earlier sense of hope started to fade. She looked at the clock on the far wall and surmised Fitzgerald would already be in his office. She reached over and picked up the phone.

*****

Adam clicked on the internet icon and waited for his home page to open. Once there, he contemplated going to CNN and checking out the news. In the past, he was a hardcore news junkie. As a world traveler, he was especially interested in the areas he had visited or might be seeing in the near future. Lately, he found the *goings on elsewhere* of little interest. He went directly to his email where thirty-nine messages waited his review. He shook his head as he started deleting those whose name or email address he didn't recognize. That cut the list in half. Next, he opened and scanned several from colleagues and friends. All basically said the same, they hoped he was doing well and to please stay in touch. He responded to each with his canned message of thank-you, yes he was doing okay and he would indeed keep in touch.

The last three were all marked urgent and were from his assistant, Carol. A faint smile crossed his face. Everything from Carol was urgent. The first message was simply a request to call her. It was the first time she had made such a request. The second message was a repeat of the first with the word please followed by a couple exclamation points. The third was a repeat of the second, this time with the word please underlined. This one also contained additional verbiage. "Daniel and the group have been evaluating a case and are having a hard time deciphering the anatomy. I think he may need your help."

The smile from a moment ago disappeared. Daniel Fitzgerald was a genius as well as a phenomenal surgeon. He also had an ego that would make Johns Hopkins frown. Adam surmised the reason the team was having difficulty was because Fitzgerald refused to ask for help outside the Hopkins Community. Adam had preached and had even given formal lectures that in all fields of medicine, one had to develop the art of critical thinking. Part of that art was knowing when to ask for assistance.

Daniel Fitzgerald had yet to get the message.

Adam stared at the screen before deleting all three emails without a response. He again contemplated going to CNN and again decided otherwise. He clicked the appropriate icons and watched the computer shut down.

He played Carol's message over in his mind. She thought Fitzgerald may need his help–a strange message to say the least. Carol was very smart and very intuitive. There wasn't much in the department that got past her. So she knew Fitzgerald needed help. But what was she really saying?

"Oh, shit," Adam said aloud as the answer came into focus. Not only was Fitzgerald too egotistical to ask for help, he didn't realize he needed it. That was the real message. "Shit," Adam repeated.

He had kept his distance from the hospital and the people there for months. He had no desire to change. Or so he kept telling himself. He didn't miss the administrative aspect of the job. He did, however, miss the actual surgery; and he missed the patients... his children.

He cut the thought off. "Don't go there," he said aloud. Fitzgerald may need him, but he certainly didn't need Fitzgerald.

*****

As the music grew louder, the gyrations on the makeshift dance floor proceeded to the point it became difficult to differentiate just who was dancing with whom–until it became clear there was no differentiation. It was just a group of people having a good time. Who was gyrating with whom was inconsequential. Adam watched in wonderment, until he remembered a ceremonial rain dance he had witnesses one night in Africa. If he remembered correctly, it even rained that night... not much, but it did rain.

He wondered if it was going to rain in Fenwick Island tomorrow.

The song, one of Ricky's upbeat tunes he had written years before, neared the finale. There was a wild flourish of guitar notes followed by loud beats from the drums. Final chords were struck and the song ended. The dancing continued a few more bars and then gradually came to a halt. A generous round of applause followed with a few whistles thrown in for good measure. Partners were recovered. Those without a partner stood around looking lost. Eventually, everyone returned to his/her designated spot at the bar and waited for the next rain dance to begin.

It was a curious phenomenon, Adam thought. No matter where you went in the world, people loved to dance. He decided it was more than a ritual. It was in mankind's genes. It was... Adam smiled and shrugged his shoulders... okay, maybe like Bobby said, it was foreplay.

He watched in silence, wondering what drew people to a place like Smitty McGee's? Did the band have that big a following? Was it the food? The drinks? The atmosphere? Or was it a combination of everything? Whatever the answer, taverns had drawn crowds through their doors for centuries. Even in the worst of times, places serving libation survived. The modern day bar was no different. And while Smitty McGee's just happened to be the bar Adam walked into that first day, there were plenty others in the area to choose from.

As he scanned the crowd, he caught his own reflection in the mirror behind the bar. What about himself, he questioned? What drew him here?

His initial visit stemmed from Mel's recommendation the first time she cut his hair. The second visit was later the same night–where he found Mel sitting at the bar. But what brought him here after that? He came. He sat. He watched. He drank.

He ate occasionally. He talked. He made barf-friends. And he spent time with Mel.

His attention was diverted as one of the regulars staggered toward the bathroom. His arms, dangling at his side, were held a good foot from his waistline. One foot was placed before the next with a sense of determination like a baby learning to walk. The man tried keeping his head up to give the aura that he was sober. He failed at that, having to look down frequently to ensure the floor was still there. He was walking a tightrope on a windy day.

And oh, there went an imaginary gust of wind as he was forced to lean against the back of a bar stool. When the gust passed, he continued his journey. He looked up and focused on the bathroom door. The end of the tightrope was in sight. Like a circus actor might do, he traveled the last few feet in a rush. The door opened and he disappeared behind it. Only unlike at the circus, there was no applause.

Turning his attention elsewhere, Adam wondered why people drank to the point of being... What was the word Bobby used? Being wasted ... fuckin' wasted, to be more precise. It was a point beyond high but before the total inability to remain upright. It was a phenomenon Adam did not understand, nor did he suspect he ever would. He had to admit he enjoyed the feeling that came along with alcohol, but he never had to walk a tightrope to the bathroom.

Adam found Bobby who was a few stools down mixing some pink concoction. Adam watched as four different liquors were poured into a silver shaker. Ice was added, the mixture shaken and then poured into three waiting long stemmed glasses which were then placed before three pretty ladies who waited with baited breath for whatever the hell it was they ordered. The last glass placed properly atop the paper cocktail napkin, Bobby gave them his signature smile. It was a smile he had refined to a fine art. Never too much. Never too little. Just the right amount to keep the ladies guessing... to keep them wondering... to keep them fantasizing about what might be.

Adam continued watching and waiting for what he knew was coming next. It only took a moment. "Would you like menus?" Bobby said. At the same time he pulled three from beneath the counter.

"Sure," all three said simultaneously.

Adam looked away before he laughed aloud. Bobby had just tripled, maybe quadrupled their bar tab for the night. A fee paid for fine art.

The doctor's attention was diverted by the drunken man's exit from the restroom. He continued to try pretending he could walk a straight line. He continued to fail. No one really seemed to pay him much mind. To Adam's amazement, the man did make it back to his designated barstool without falling on his face. His wife, who had just come off the dance floor, was waiting for him with a wet kiss. Also waiting was a shot glass of cloudy liquid, which he swallowed in one gulp. Adam shook his head side to side. He figured that as long as you could climb back up onto your barstool, you could still get a drink.

It was the ninth wonder of the world.

Suddenly, the lights flickered. A bolt of lightning sparkled across the sky. A clap of thunder shook the building. By the time the vibrations stopped, you could hear the rain on the roof. Adam looked over at the band. The next song was just beginning. The rain dancers were starting to dance, even though they had already done their job. Adam's smile widened. The tenth wonder of the world.

Then as an afterthought, he asked himself, "Just how many other wonders of the world were out there?"

*****

"Look around you," Bobby said, waving an arm side to side. "All you see are smiles, laughter and joy. Smitty McGee's is a place to go to be happy. Very seldom do you see someone here down in the dumps. Sure, we get the occasional broken hearted female–Doug seems to attract those women, but overall..."

"Why is that?" Adam asked as he raised his glass to his lips.

"We don't allow it," Bobby replied. "Our job is to bring pleasure to people, not sorrow. People come here to buy happiness."

Adam took another big drink. "You're forgetting something."

"And that is?"

Adam emptied his glass. The first of the day always seemed to go quickly. "Money can't buy happiness. It may buy happy things, but not the emotion itself."

"Words of wisdom," Bobby said.

Adam ignored the sarcasm. Instead, he started, "words of..." He cut the sentence off. He slid the empty glass forward. When the refill was complete, he continued. "Happiness is something that has to be earned, developed, molded, allowed to ferment like a fine wine. It can't be rushed. Rushing is asking for trouble."

Bobby's facial expression changed. The sarcasm left his voice. "Very profound." Unlike his normal action of making such a comment and then disappearing, he stayed put. His head tilted to the side. "You really are a very wise man, Doc."

Adam smiled and said. "You are, too, my friend."

*****

The door opened, carrying in a big gust of wind, and on its back a blanket of rain. At the same time, a streak of lightning lit up the darkened sky followed by the sound of thunder. The person responsible for the intrusion pulled the door shut, holding it a moment to make sure it was going to stay latched. Satisfied, the figure, without a coat and soaked to the skin, turned and faced the bar. Bobby, who was now wiping up the spray that had blown across the freshly polished wood, stared and said, "look what the wind blew in. Don't you have an umbrella, Adam?"

Taking the towel that had been tossed his way, Adam said, "No I do not, and I doubt it would do much good either. Besides, it wasn't supposed to rain today."

"Hell, man, this is the beach. It can rain here any day, any time, regardless what the forecasters say."

"It doesn't matter," Adam said. "I imagine it'll be over soon now that I'm inside."

"You think the storm was after you, huh?"

"Had to be. I was the only one out there."

Both men looked out the window, and sure enough, the storm was starting to abate. Bobby laughed. He stepped away and returned with two shots of B&B. Sliding one towards Adam, he said,

"Here, this'll warm you up some."

"What makes you think I'm cold?"

"You will be soon. Sunny had the AC recharged this morning. Supposed to hit eighty today."

Glasses were clicked, the bar tapped and the liquor was downed. Handing Adam another towel, Bobby said, "Look at it this way, Adam. How often do you get to exercise and take a shower at the same time?"

Adam laughed–at Bobby and himself. It felt good. He laughed harder. It felt even better. Then like the storm, the laughter subsided. It had been a long time since he had been caught in the rain. It had been a long time since he had laughed so hard. It subsided, replaced by another emotion... another feeling... unclear, out of focus, different, a bit strange... in the distance perhaps, like faint claps of thunder, but there nonetheless.

He looked up at Bobby as he ran a towel through his hair. "Got any shampoo?"

*****

Doug came over shaking his head side to side. "You know, Adam, we have the hardest working bar backs in the business. But man, some are dumber than an onion." He motioned to where Kevin, one of the most senior members of the team, was washing glasses. The bartender continued. "He got a call from an ex-girlfriend last night saying she wanted to hang out and talk. Well, lover boy here didn't drive himself to work. Seems he was on the wheels of a new girlfriend he'd just met a week or so ago. She's a little airy in the head, if you know what I mean–an IQ one point below a corn stalk. But she does have the body. Anyway, Kevin told me about the call, and I told him not to even think about it."

"So what does stupid here do? He asks the new one to drive him over to the bar where the old one was waiting... and he told her why. Not knowing any better herself, airhead takes him. Then later, she catches him sucking face with the old one. Now how stupid is that?"

Just then, Kevin came by. Doug smacked him with a towel. "Dumb ass. Kids these days, they just don't listen."

*****

It was late. Last call was only minutes away. Adam had been sitting next to Marvin, one of the older regulars he had gotten to know over these many months. Marvin was a retired insurance salesman from Philadelphia and had moved down to the area with his wife. His wife usually came in with him. Tonight, she stayed home to watch a movie. "Something about vampires," Marvin said.

Someone in return noted that vampires would like Smitty McGee's.

"Why's that?" Marvin bit.

"Because they have a Bloody Mary bar on the weekends." Marvin laughed and promised everyone he'd tell his wife.

That was earlier. Now, Marvin's attention was on two young men sitting across from him. Both wore crew cut hair, both were clean shaven and both had what could simply be described as hard bodies. Their conversation gave away they were both in the Marines, presently on leave.

Now Marvin was never one to keep much to himself. He came to the bar like most people would come to the kitchen table–for food, drink and conversation. Like at the kitchen table, any conversation was open for interruption, which Marvin practiced frequently–including this night. He said loudly, yet politely. "Can I ask you gentlemen something?"

The two Marines stopped talking and looked his way. The one on the left served as spokesman for the duo. "Go ahead."

Marvin nodded and said, "Why is it that you military guys have to do so many push-ups?"

The spokesman spoke without hesitation. "Push-ups help make us strong, so we are better in battle. You know, we can carry up to sixty pounds of gear, sometimes even more."

"That so?"

The spokesperson nodded.

"Bullshit," the non-spokesperson said rather curtly.

"Bullshit?" Marvin said. "How's that?"

"Has nothing to do with going into battle. They make us do push-ups so we're strong when we go out on leave."

"How do push-ups help you there?" Marvin asked.

"For fuc... for lovemaking," the non-spokesperson said.

Marvin's bushy eyebrows raised high into the air. "For lovemaking?"

The Marine hesitated. "No disrespect, sir, but let me explain it to you this way." He pointed toward one of the waitresses who was cleaning up in preparation for the end of her shift. "If you were a beautiful woman like that girl over there, who would you rather have over top of you–an old out of shape fart like you who can probably do one, maybe two push-ups at the most, or someone like me who can do fifty without raising my heart rate? Again, no disrespect, sir."

Marvin, having grown very wise over the years as a salesman, knew when further conversation was fruitless. "No disrespect taken, son," he said. He motioned for Doug to set the Marines up with beers on him.

Last call was thirty seconds away.

Behind Bars

Doug, as he tended to do, was standing in front of several ladies. They had been going back and forth over the past couple hours, arguing everything from music to politics. And as conversations with Doug tended to do with the ladies, the topic eventually found its way around to relationships. Doug stayed on message that in his opinion, the best relationship was one that was open-ended for both parties, arguing that variety was the spice of life. The ladies, one of whom was getting married soon, countered that his argument was simply a cop out for an unwillingness to make a commitment. To which he countered that a commitment could be made to have an open ended relationship.

One of the bridesmaids looked at the bartender and said, "Tell me, Doug, have you ever been in love... and I mean true love, not lust?"

Doug looked at her. "Yes."

"During that time, did you feel the way you do now?"

As the bartender pondered the point, he said, "Good question. I don't really know."

"Exactly," the bridesmaid argued. "When you're in love, you're focused. It's when you're out of love, your mind starts to wander."

"Are you focused? Or are you so infatuated you

can't think of anything else?" Doug countered. "Here's how I think it should go. When you start a relationship, take each other out for a test drive. If that works out, then maybe a short-term lease. Anything more is just too risky."

The girl smiled. "You're a pig, you know that? You live in a fantasy world and nothing can change that."

"Is that so bad?" the bartender asked, a thread of defensiveness in his voice.

The girl's smile continued. "There's more to life than fantasy, Doug."

"And what might that be?"

"Reality," she spouted. "Your mind may be in fantasy land, but life is real."

"I never said it wasn't," Doug argued. "Just remember, many people survive the reality of life through the world of fantasy. Take you for instance, look how you're dressed. All made up, fancy earrings, a low cut blouse, your boobs held up by one of those fancy expensive bras. You're wearing a skirt that comes up to the bottom of your butt." He leaned forward. "And you're wearing a perfume that doesn't even come close to what you really smell like. So what world are you living in? And maybe more importantly, what world do you want the person looking at you to be living in? If you're not dressed up to create a fantasy in someone's mind, I don't know what you are. But that's okay, because fantasy naked is

235

always better than reality naked."

The bridesmaid opened and closed her mouth. Finally, "it works both ways."

"I never said it didn't. Then again, I didn't call you a pig, either."

Again, her mouth opened without emitting any sound.

Doug leaned in toward the still silent girl. "Yes, fantasy naked is better than reality naked, but I suspect in your case, the two are close?"

A smile crossed her face. "You really are a pig... but a sweet pig."

Doug let out a loud laugh. "I've been called a lot of things before, but never a sweet pig."

"Don't press your luck," the girl warned.

Across the way, three older men, Adam included, were listening to the conversation with keen interest. "I got ten bucks he'll have her in the sack before the night's over," one said.

"I wouldn't bet against that," the other man said.

Adam sat there and smiled. After a moment, he said, "I think you have the fish and fisherman mixed up there," he said.

The two other men looked at one another and then at the doctor. "You think she's the one going after him?"

"She set him up from the moment she called him a pig. That's not something you usually say with a smile on your face," Adam suggested.

The other two men nodded in unison. "Think we *oughta* alert ole' Dougie boy there?" one said.

"Nah," Adam said. "The end result's going to be the same either way."

"Yeah," the one man chuckled. "He's going to get laid, and we're not."

"I don't know," the other man said. "The blonde there looks ripe for picking."

"That's the bride-to-be."

"So?"

"Now who's the pig?"

*****

One only had to look up and down the bar to see it was going to be a beer crowd kind of night. There's nothing wrong with beer drinkers, except their tabs tended to be lower. Regardless, the beer flowed freely, the music was loud, and Ricky sang on with the entire band around him. The crowd was lively; the area in front of the band was crowded with sweat pouring off the faces of those dancing.

Adam, who was sitting in the corner across from the band, saw Sunny come out of her office to check on things. She made her way up and down the bar, saying 'hi' to everyone and stopping to chat with a few. Her eyes, however, never stopped recording what was going on around her.

Bobby came up and gave her a glass of wine. She took it with a nod and then leaned over and said something to Bobby, who turned and faced the band. Catching Ricky's attention, he held up three fingers.

Ricky nodded and continued the song. "So many dreams we threw away. So many words we meant to say..." When the song was finished and the applause subsided, he stepped up to the microphone and spoke loudly, "Folks, I've just been informed that for the next thirty minutes, Sunny's offering three dollar shots." As he finished, a shot of Jim Beam was passed his way. He downed it in a gulp and said, "good stuff, folks. Remember to tip your bar and wait staff." Then the music started to play again.

Needless to say, there was a flurry of orders that kept the bartenders busy a while. When Bobby finally got over to Adam with a shot of B&B, he said, "Works every time."

"In medicine, it's called giving out samples," Adam said.

Bobby nodded and looked over his shoulder to make sure Sunny was preoccupied. Then he quickly downed a shot of his own. "Tastes like medicine to me," he said as he hurried to refill a line of beer mugs that were suddenly empty.

*****

"You know, Adam, you and me are different in many ways, but we also have a lot in common."

"How's that?" Adam asked, his curiosity flag rising.

"We each have children we don't really want, but we love 'em to death anyway."

"Huh?"

Bobby continued. "I have my niece and nephew. You have your patients."

"That may be true for you, Bobby," Adam started to argue. "But..."

Bobby held up his hand to cut the verbiage short. "Don't even pretend," he directed. "You may be able to say no for now, but never for ever."

"What makes you say that?" Adam asked.

"Like I said, in spite of our differences, we have similarities. And if your next question is to name one, it's really quite simple–we both give a damn."

Then he was gone.

*****

"Here's one for the book," Bobby said to Adam one night as he stopped by with a refill. "No one in the bar business is faithful, and all cops are crooked."

"That's certainly a sad state of affairs," Adam commented.

"Maybe... maybe not. Depends on your perspective, I guess. But here's another one," Bobby said. "I saw a guy cutting coke at the bar one day... right on top of the bar mind you. So I came up and simply blew the powder onto the floor. The guy wasn't very happy with me until I pointed several stools down to a group of men who luckily hadn't noticed the odd behavior. 'Fenwick's version of a narc squad,' I said. The man still wasn't very happy. He left a good tip though."

"You ever see him again?" Adam asked.

"Nope, and don't expect to, either."

"Why's that?"

"He's dead. Ran off the road a week later." Bobby paused. "You be careful out there... walking home at night, you hear?"

Adam nodded. "I always am."

*****

Bobby wandered up to a group of locals nursing their beers, except for Adam who was chewing on ice basted in whisky. "None of you guys were here the other night," the bartender said. "But right around 10:00, a young girl and her mother came in. They sat where you guys are now. Both smelled of smoke, like they had just come from a fire or something. Anyway, the mother drops a burned up wallet on top the bar along with a burned up birth certificate. The daughter says, 'Today's my 21st birthday. My mother and I were on our way here to celebrate. She wanted to be the first person to buy me a drink. But on the way here our car caught on fire. I got my mother and dog out, but I forgot my purse. That's all that's left.' She pointed to the burned papers smelling up the bar. 'I am twenty one. Today's my birthday–for real. Can I please have a beer?'

"I returned a few seconds later with three Heinies–two for them and one for me. I raised my bottle and wished her happy birthday. They were all smiles the rest of the night. Left a good tip, too."

"What about numbers?" one of the locals said, "did you get her telephone number?"

"Nah, she was a little young for me."

"Since when is twenty-one too young for anyone?" another local laughed.

Bobby stared the man in the eye. A smile formed as he patted his shirt pocket. "I did get the mother's number, though."

*****

Bobby pointed to an old guy who had just bellied up to the bar, literally and figuratively. The bartender said, "Now there's a guy who's been coming in here for years–maybe once a week, sometimes twice. He sits down and throws a $20 bill on the bar, and asks for a menu and a draft. We call him the twenty dollar man. He tells us to cut him off at fifteen dollars. That leaves five for us." Bobby paused as he watched Sunny go up to him with a menu and a draft. The $20 bill was already out on the counter. "Been doing that for years," Bobby said, shaking his head gently side to side.

Later, a female patron with big boobs covered by a thin halter top walked by just as Bobby was replacing Adam's empty glass. Not worrying whether she was out of earshot or not, he said, "now that's what we call a set of eye wiggles."

"Eye wiggles?" Adam repeated, turning and looking at the objects in question.

"Yeah, her boobs are bouncing up and down so much they cause your eyes to do the same, and then you get dizzy. Why, I've even seen men fall off their bar stools when an eye wiggler goes by."

Adam laughed, "We have a term for that in medicine. It's called nystagmus." "So, she's causing a real medical condition, huh?"

Adam laughed louder. "Seems that way."

"Then maybe we should ban her from the bar... you know, for health reasons and what not."

"Nah, I wouldn't do that," Adam objected. "They've got pills for things like that."

"For that?" Bobby nodded to where the girl was now scooting a stool up to the bar. That action alone caused additional dizziness in the patrons who were watching.

"We've got pills for everything, Bobby."

"Do you now?" the bartender said. He turned and walked in the direction of the newest customer.

Later that night, a woman, who normally drank Budweiser from a bottle with a shot of vodka on the side, ordered a scotch and water. Little caused Bobby to hesitate, but this request did, as the woman, in her 50's and a cougar at heart, was a longtime customer and had been drinking the same combination for years. Serving up a scotch and water, Bobby said, "Why the change?"

The woman took a sip of the liquid, made a face as the unfamiliar liquor burned her throat, made another face as the after taste kicked in, and then said, "I'm on Weight Watchers."

Just then, a couple of patrons who'd been outside smoking piled back in laughing, not hysterically, but close to it. One of them said, "some guy out there just fell off the bulkhead into the fuckin' water."

"How the hell'd he do that?" someone said.

"Fuck if I know," the guy said.

Sunny, who happened to be walking by, paused and said, "there's only one reason some bloke who's out back falls into the water."

Everyone thought about it and then there was a collective laugh.

Adam laughed too. Then he realized there was something interesting and wrong with this picture... something very interesting. Not one person inquired about the well-being of the man who fell in the water.

The twenty dollar man, a young thing with wiggles, a cougar on Weight Watchers and a poor bloke simply trying to take a leak... such was life at the bar.

Adam grabbed a napkin and a pen. He wrote the stories down and then hesitated as a thought came to mind. Being careful not to tear the flimsy writing tablet, he added:

It writes itself.

18

End of May 2009

Bobby looked up as the door chimes rang. He watched the newest customer pause as her eyes adjusted to the darker environment. She had that easy to recognize *this is my first time here* look about her. Bobby's hand subconsciously went through his hair, his other hand smoothed out his shirt. Before she had even chosen a seat, he was in front of her, the famous smile plastered across his face. "Afternoon. Welcome to Smitty McGee's... I'm Bobby. What can I get you?" He slid a cocktail napkin in front of her.

"Hello," she said in return, continuing her visual reconnaissance.

Bobby quickly concluded that besides this being her first time to Smitty's, she was here with a purpose–she was looking for someone. And from Bobby's many years of experience, a single woman coming into a bar looking for someone usually meant trouble.

She was easy on the eyes, mid-thirties maybe, medium height, shoulder length brown hair, a smooth face, a short stubby nose that sported librarian type glasses, gold dangling earrings, and a neck that led to quite a stunning body. As was Bobby's practice when undergoing such an important piece of surveillance, he didn't picture her naked. Instead, he pictured her on the beach in a bikini–a much better way, in his opinion, to judge someone. He immediately decided he liked the picture.

Her purview of the place completed, she met his stare, luckily just as his eyes returned to her face. "Diet Coke, please."

He figured as much. Good to look at, but a cheap tab. But he had ways around that. As he set her soda on the napkin, he pulled a menu from beneath the counter. "Hungry?"

She hesitated, which told him the answer was affirmative so he continued. "We have a chicken salad sandwich on special today. It's a new recipe we just started serving last week. It's been a big seller so far."

She nodded yes. "Rye toast. Lettuce and tomato. No extra mayo."

"Wanna run a tab?" he asked.

"Sure."

"Name?"

She smiled. "Just my name?"

"That's enough... for now."

"Carol... Carol Johnston."

"Okay, Carol." He nodded and stepped away to put in the order.

When her food was ready, he placed it in front of her and refilled her soda. "Let me know if you need anything," he said. He moved away but kept her in the corner of his eye. She attacked the sandwich heartily. He guessed she had driven a good way to get here. She definitely wasn't a local. Dressed in a white blouse and tan skirt, she was too businesslike. Adam refreshed his earlier image of her in a bikini, and reminded himself she was probably on a search and rescue mission, so curiosity was okay as long as it came with a good dose of caution.

When she was finished eating, he went over and cleared her dish. Wiping off the counter, he said casually, "so, what brings you to these parts?"

She didn't back away from the inquiry. Instead, "is this the only Smitty McGee's around here?"

"The original and the only."

"Then do you know an Adam Singer... Dr. Adam Singer?"

Bobby paused in his wiping. He had been right, she was on the prowl. The target of her search, however, came as a surprise.

His hesitation was enough for Carol to get her answer. "He usually comes here in the evenings, right?"

Bobby's eyes widened. "How would you know that?"

She sat up straight and gave the bartender a

reassuring look. "Answer my question then I'll answer yours."

Not wanting to chase her away, at the same time not wanting to reveal too much, he spoke cautiously. "Yes, he comes mostly in the evenings, although he stops in for lunch or happy hour now and then."

"Thank you," she said.

"You're welcome." There was a moment's silence. "So," Bobby added.

"So?"

"I answered your question. Now you answer mine."

"Which was?"

Bobby straightened up. "Just who the hell are you?"

Again, she didn't react the way he expected. Instead, "one more question first. You obviously know him, but do you know who he is and what he is?"

"If you mean do I know he's a world famous neurosurgeon..."

"Pediatric neurosurgeon," she quickly corrected.

Bobby broke into a laugh. "You're a chip off the old block, aren't you?"

She returned the smile. "It's just that he's sensitive about that."

"Don't I know?" Bobby let some of his defensiveness abate. "Yes, I know who he is and what he is."

Carol's eyebrows rose. "How much do you know?"

Bobby leaned forward and spoke gently. "Who are you?"

She smiled. "I'm a chip off the ole block." She let out a long breath. At the same time, her expression turned serious. "I'm his administrative assistant. I've been with him since he finished his fellowship. I've traveled with him all over the world... and no, I'm not his lover. But I am probably closer to him than anyone since his wife died. I know he comes here because I take care of his personal matters. I was supposed to be the godmother to his and Nancy's child." She looked away. "I was outside the operating room in Africa the last time he came out of surgery."

"You, and a whole lot of bad news," Bobby said. He refilled her soda. "Heavy bars."

"Huh?"

"Another time."

She wiped her eyes. "Anyway, I... we've all been worried about him. He's been gone for so long and doesn't respond to any of our emails except to say that he's okay. That was fine for a while, but now, the hospital..."

Bobby waited a second before picking up the conversation. "Now the hospital wants their golden boy back."

"They have been very patient," she argued.

"I'm sure they have, but there comes a time when patience runs out."

She tipped her head slightly to the side. "You know, for a bartender, you're a very smart man."

Bobby laughed. "I have my moments." He paused. "So you came down here to find him and knock some sense into his head?"

"I just want to make sure he's okay."

Something outside caught Bobby's eye. "What would it be worth to you to see him and find that out for yourself?" he said.

"What would you want for that?" she asked cautiously.

He gave her a half smile. "How about dinner?"

She returned the expression. "Bobby dear, please don't take this the wrong way, but it would be worth a whole lot more than that."

The door opened and the chimes rang. "I get off at seven tonight. I'll meet you back here, say seven-thirty?"

"A little presumptuous, aren't we?"

"Seven-thirty sharp," he said, pointing toward the door.

Carol turned. Her mouth dropped open. Her throat threatened to close. He looked so thin, so frail. He had lost an awful lot of weight. She sat there and stared.

*****

Adam pushed open the door and waited for his eyes to adjust to the dark. He did a quick look around and saw Bobby standing with his hands flattened out on the bar. He started to wave, but stopped. The bartender had a very odd expression on his face. Then Adam looked a little to the left and saw why.

*****

Adam stared at his half empty glass, eyes unfocused. His thoughts swirled like bees over clover. Only unlike the well-organized dance of the honey bees, he was confused and conflicted. He now had to do something he had not done in a long time. He had to make a decision... a major decision.

He finally looked up at Carol, who had not taken her eyes off him since he first walked into the bar. Even as Bobby quickly ushered them into the back area, she remained close at his side, obviously afraid he was going to turn and run away. He assured her that wouldn't be the case, even though that's exactly what he felt like doing. Bobby brought a round of drinks and left them alone. Carol did most of the talking.

She went through the expected oration that everybody was worried sick about him and everybody sent their wishes. She also told him the hospital was putting pressure on Daniel Fitzgerald to either get Adam back on board or get a replacement. The hospital administration had been very supportive, but they felt the need to move forward. Adam couldn't complain, and in spite of a small wave of anger, he fully understood the hospital's position. After all, they had left him alone until now.

But Carol didn't have to come down here to tell him all that. There was something else. Taking a sip of his drink, he said in a soft yet firm voice, "why are you really here, Carol?"

"Like I told you, I wanted to make sure you were okay and to let you know about the hospital issue."

"Emails have been working so far," he pointed out bluntly.

"Yes, but..." She met his hard stare, at first with a nervous expression, then with the calmness and professionalism he had grown to expect from her. As bluntly as he had spoken a moment ago, she spoke to him, "Fitz needs your help."

Adam laughed nervously. "That would certainly be a first."

"Don't be too hard on him, Adam. He's done a commendable job at keeping everything together while you've been away."

"I have no doubt he has," Adam said smugly. "And I'm sure he's more than willing to take over the department, at a great sacrifice to himself I might add, if I don't come back." He kept the question to himself whether Fitzgerald was the driving force behind the hospital's supposed interest in moving on.

"He doesn't know he needs your help, Adam," Carol said. "That's why I'm here. I didn't want to take the chance of talking about this over the internet. Besides, you didn't answer my emails."

Adam stared at his assistant. His instinct about Fitzgerald had been right. "Tell me what you've got," he finally said.

Carol leaned forward in her chair. "There's a case of conjoined twins down in South America the UCLA group is looking at. They've consulted with us for an opinion. The twins are joined at the head and there's something about the complexity of the blood vessels they can't decipher. Our guys have been working on it and have similar questions. Fitz being Fitz admits this, but is planning to go ahead and advise surgery anyway, saying they will get a lot more information once they get into the brain."

Adam didn't have to tell Carol that this was a very dangerous strategy. Meticulous preparation was the key to avoid going in blindfolded, and still there were surprises. "What do they say out there?" Adam said, referring to the UCLA group. Adam knew them well. They were an up and coming team, yet lacked the experience of the Hopkins group.

"They're anxious to hone their skills, Adam. So they're probably gullible to do whatever Fitzgerald says."

"You think it's too risky?" Adam queried.

Carol smiled. "Nice try, boss. You know I'm not a doctor. All I know is there's a conflict... and you may be able to help."

Adam let a smile cross his face, the first since he and Carol were reunited. "Touché."

Carol reached down and pulled a computer disc from her purse. "Here's a copy of the MRI and angiogram. Take a look and make your own judgment. I put the meeting schedule on it as well." She slid the disc across the table.

As Adam stared at the table, his mind was already kicking into gear. There was also something else he couldn't put his finger on. He didn't have time to think about it as the curtain opened and Bobby slid through.

"Don't mean to interrupt guys, but I just wanted to check and see if you need anything," the bartender said.

"I think we're okay," Carol said.

"Well, if you do, Sunny and Doug are both here. Things are slow, so I'm cutting out early."

"That's a little unusual for you isn't it?" Adam said.

Bobby gave one of his smiles. Even in the darkened room, his glowed. "I've got to go home and get ready."

Adam took the bait. "Ready for what?"

"I have a date tonight."

"You have a what!" Adam said, failing to hide his surprise.

Bobby ignored the comment and looked down at Carol. "Seven-thirty, remember?"

For the first time in a long time, the administrative assistant of the world renowned pediatric neurosurgeon blushed.

19

June, 2009

From your friendly bartender:

There's not a vegetable you can't make a bowl out of.

The liquor Gentlemen's Jack is certainly no gentleman the next morning.

Never trust a skinny cook.

Bobby's favorite tee shirt logo: *I can fix anything. Where's the duct tape*?

*****

Bobby reached into the cooler and pulled out a bottle of Coke–one of those old 6½ ounce bottles you rarely see. He popped the cap, took a long swig and said, "best soda ever made... and no, it doesn't taste the same as it used to."

"Nothing tastes like it used to," someone a few stools down said.

"Bullshit," an older patron added. "I've been drinking Jack longer than you've been alive, and I ain't noticed a difference."

"Regardless, I don't think Bobby has Coke in

that bottle anyway. You ever notice when he pops the cap, you never hear the fizz."

All eyes turned to Bobby for an explanation, who responded by winking at his audience. "You'll never know, will ya?" And then he was gone.

"That's one boy who ain't changed since I've known him," someone said.

Adam, who had wisely remained quiet during this conversation, suspected the last comment to be wrong. He strongly suspected Bobby had indeed changed over the years... at least over the past few years. Responsibilities for children...

He cut the thought off as he caught his own reflection in the back mirror.

Responsibilities for children... He looked away and closed his eyes.

Ricky announced they were going to do their last song for the evening. As they often did, the band ended with a patriotic medley. A favorite was *I'm Proud to be an American*. It usually stimulated the crowd to stand and sing along. Adam stood with the crowd and wondered how he had changed over these many months. He wondered why he should be proud. In the past, there were many reasons, but at this juncture in his life...

"God bless the USA," Ricky sang.

Adam finished his drink, dropped some money on the bar and slid out the back door.

*****

Adam sat quietly watching the Buzztime questions come up. He didn't know the category of this particular game, but he wasn't doing very well. So far he was 0 for 8. Mel, on the other hand, was doing quite well, which wasn't a surprise. The more time Adam spent with her, the more he realized just how special she was. Not only was she a trivia whiz, she was intelligent in general. There were other attributes as well, such as a gentle calmness she carried with her. It was a calmness that often trickled over to him, bringing a warmth he had not felt in a long time.

Ricky and the band were playing. Aided by several rounds of beer and bourbon, they gave the patrons what they wanted–entertainment. Entertained patrons tended to forget the problems in the world, the problems in their community, the problems in one's life. Entertainment at places such as Smitty's functioned as a buffer zone, a time to forget the negatives and focus on the positives, a time to put away the tears, a time to bring out the cheer. It also served another purpose. For couples who were in love or headed that way, it was the artist's canvas for what was to come.

As the lone couple on the floor danced to the next slow tune.

They danced ever so closely. So close, Adam

wondered how they could move. She was thin and medium height with curled brown shoulder length hair. She was dressed in a decorative white top and tight jeans. Her feet were covered by a pair of high heeled shoes. Her partner, several inches taller, was bald and somewhat overweight. He wore a black tee shirt with a fishing logo on the back and a pair of not-so-tight jeans. His feet were in work boots. They danced with her hands around his neck, his hands buried deep in the rear pockets of her jeans. It didn't matter that they were out of time with the music. The only thing important was that they were together, dancing, enjoying their emotions and anticipating what was to come. Soon other couples joined them.

"Foreplay," Adam muttered.

"What did you say?" Mel queried, his voice distracting her from her game.

Adam blushed at being caught talking aloud. "Nothing," he said.

She looked in the direction of his stare, a smile forming on her face. "That it is," she agreed. "That it is." She kissed him on the shoulder and returned to her game.

The music stopped. Applause broke out. Ricky spewed out a line of thank you's and acknowledged the band. Beers were sipped and another round of shots were delivered. Adam looked at the table behind the band that was already full of empty beer bottles. The windowsill was full of empty shot glasses. Adam wondered if he should buy some stock in Jim Beam.

Ricky introduced a special guest for the evening. He was a tall thin man with long dirty blond hair. Adam guessed he was in his thirties. He wore a plain white tee shirt, dark khaki pants and sandals. He had a nice smile about him and nodded to the crowd as he approached the band. Ricky handed him his guitar and stepped back. The singer stepped up to the mike and spoke softly, "thank you, Ricky. Thank you everyone. I'd like to do a song from my new CD *Ohio*. It's called *The Song I Wished I Wrote*."

He turned and looked at the other members of the band who had returned to their places. "Let's do it in the key of C," he said.

The man had one of those gravely country/bluegrass/rock voices that tended to catch one's attention. Adam could only think of the word unique as a way of describing it. He listened as the song began... in the key of C.

But the song that I wish I wrote
Is one where you stay.
And I'm not hanging on
Mistakes that I've made.
And maybe there'd still be time
And something to say
In the song that I wish I wrote

Behind Bars

The one where you stay.

The song finished without the normal flurry of guitar strums and drum rolls. It just seemed to dissipate into the air like a tornado rising back into the heavens. And then like the calm after a storm, there was a moment of quietness, followed by spontaneous, loud applause. The guest singer looked as if he was about to blush.

Adam added his own to the applause before turning to face the trivia game. He tried to focus, but instead, could only replay the lyrics he had just heard.

Then he replayed them again and added a few of his own.

The song I wish I wrote.
The story I wish I told.
The stop I wish I made.
The woman I wished I loved.
The touch I wish I gave.

He looked at Mel, who looked his way. She smiled, her teeth shining in the light. She leaned over and gave him a kiss on the cheek. He glowed in return. She went back to her game. She was now the leader and the next question had just arrived. He looked at the question and had no clue as to the answer. He put his arm across the back of her chair. There was a moment's hesitation.

The touch I wish I gave.

His hand lifted off the wood and flattened across her back. His fingers gently caressed the material of her blouse. He pressed harder, until he could feel the smoothness of her skin. He gently messaged the area. She looked at him and silently mouthed, "that feels good." She turned back to her game.

His attention returned to the couple on the dance floor who were waiting for the next song to begin. "Foreplay," he thought. "That would be a good name for a bar."

20

Middle of June

The next day, Adam sat with the recliner part way back, his neck flexed forward so he could see out the patio door. The tallest tree at the edge of the woods swayed back and forth as a stiff breeze blew off Dirickson Creek. While the foundation for the house behind him had been poured the day before, the lumber had yet to arrive. When it did, Adam knew his view would be quickly lost.

His thoughts returned to the night before. There had been plenty of people at Smitty McGee's, including the usual cadre of barfriends. He and Mel sat in their regular spot, drank their normal beverage and ate their usual food. There was really nothing unusual about the evening. During the trek home, however, something started gnawing at the back of his mind, and continuing this morning. He closed his eyes and tried to focus.

It didn't take him long to remember. It was a song Ricky sang. No, it wasn't Ricky; it was that other guy... the guest singer. The words from the song came to him.

The song I wish I wrote... the story I wish I told.
Adam's thoughts stopped abruptly. He shook his head. His mind refocused on the scene outside. Suddenly, everything became quite clear.

*****

Adam walked slowly, his hands behind his back, the gentle breeze blowing at his face. He could smell the mist off the ocean. It was a fragrance like no other. He took in a couple of deep breaths as he continued down the Boardwalk. The old weathered slats felt good beneath his feet. The sound of the wood responding to his weight brought back fond memories. He took in the sights as he walked. There were plenty of people about, and in spite of the temperature hovering in the mid 60's, there were people out on the beach. He smiled figuring these people had come to Ocean City for an early vacation and were going to the beach, regardless.

In his early years, it was nothing to walk the two plus miles from one end to the other several times a night. Since coming to the Boardwalk the past month, however, he never made it to the end, always turning around at the firefighter's memorial. That was far enough, he argued. In reality, it was simply an excuse... an excuse not to go where the memories might not be so pleasant.

Today, however, he passed the memorial with little trepidation. It was such a beautiful day, he argued. Why not go all the way?

The lyrics from the night before crossed his mind. *The song I wish I wrote... the story I wish I told.*

To keep his mind off what lay ahead, he continued to focus on the activity around him. In front was a lady speaking French to the man whose arm she was clinging to as she strutted forward–stumbling in a pair of high platform shoes. Perfect footwear for the Boardwalk, Adam thought. A short time later, a man jogged by followed by a teenager on a skateboard. As several people peddled on modern day bicycles, Adam wondered whatever happened to the old Boardwalk bikes. He missed the old style two wheelers.

On the beach, two people were running through the sand, a difficult thing to do. Leading was a short petite yet strongly built girl striding along, her rhythm well controlled. Behind her was a much taller, heavier young man about the same age. He may have been in shape in the past, but now he was obviously struggling. They both wore red sweatshirts with a white cross on the front and matching sweat pants. Adam watched and wondered when the physical test for the Ocean City lifeguards was scheduled and if the girl had enough time to whip her partner into shape.

Adam passed a group of elderly couples. They

had obviously not been to Ocean City before as they were pointing at everything they saw and ducking every time a sea gull dive bombed their stash of fries. They spoke in German, shouting to one another as they decided upon a strategy to deal with the pesky birds. Adam wanted to tell them the only way to keep the birds at bay was to toss the food out on the beach. But like a good local, he kept his mouth shut. Besides, what would a trip to the ocean be without a little bird shit on your head?

Adam turned his attention to the multitude of shops around him. Many businesses had changed, but old favorites were still there. Fisher's Popcorn was open, the back area filled with workers cranking out the famous caramel snack. The Old Time Photo shop was open as well, and even had a couple picking out the costume they were going to wear. Thrasher's had the inevitable line of people waiting for fries. Adam couldn't remember the last time he had been on the Boardwalk when there wasn't a line of people there. Ripley's was open, as were several of the carnival type amusements–the ones where you pay your money to win an overstuffed animal. There were food stands. There were tee shirt and souvenir shops, each with the obligatory tank of hermit crabs in front. Jewelry stores selling gold by the inch were prevalent as well. Emotions improving, he thought maybe he should go in and get a new watch. "Maybe later," he mouthed. He slowed his pace as he approached Playland. He remembered in his early years standing at the counter for what seemed like hours trying to decide what prizes to get in exchange for his hard earned tickets. He'd heard there was a fire the week before. It appeared to have been contained to the south end of the building. If he remembered correctly, the area was where the skeeball games were housed. He always liked to play skeeball. Passing Dumser's ice cream stand, he contemplated stopping for a strawberry shake, but decided later for that as well.

Side stepping a group of low rider bikes, he took a couple of deep breaths and continued forward. Another minute brought him to the lifesaving museum. He hesitated, but only for a moment. He had come this far. Why stop now?

He ignored the range of possible answers.

He walked around the display of world record fish and stared out across the water. The wind was coming from the south and the tide was ebbing so there was a fair chop coming through the inlet. He watched a couple of small fishing boats plow their way through the rough water. They were followed by a commercial boat that sprayed water with every rise and fall. Adam looked at the benches angled for maximum view. He'd noticed that along the main section of the Boardwalk, the old concrete and wood benches had been replaced with newer, metal framed models. He leaned forward and looked at the plaque on one. It was one of those *In Memory Of* plaques.

He headed into an area of small shops off the main Boardwalk, strolling past the array of store fronts, checking the windows as a way of stalling for time. He turned and faced Harrison's Seafood Restaurant. He could smell the mixture of aromas coming from the kitchen in the back. The smells aroused his hunger which had been dormant most of the day. The smells awoke other sensations as well. He imagined he could hear her. He imagined he could feel her. He imagined he could see her. He let the memories consume him more than they had in months.

His pace quickened as he moved deeper into the complex of stores. Another hundred feet and he rounded the end of the building. He kept his eyes focused on the water. He had a sudden fear it wasn't going to be there, replaced like all the others. What if it wasn't there? What would he do? The knots in his stomach tightened. He took several steps forward, continuing to look straight ahead. He stopped, closed his eyes and like the lifeguard in training a few minutes before, sucked in several deep breaths. He opened his eyes and looked down.

The old wooden bench was still there.

It was their bench... the one where so many important things in their life had been decided or planned. It looked weathered and old, but it always looked that way. He imagined splinters ready to attack anyone who dared to sit. His eyes filled with tears.

Months had passed–over a year. And now here he was, back where so much of his life had started. This was the site of their first kiss. This is where he asked her to be his wife. This is where they came when they had other major decisions to make. The bench had always been there for them. It was still waiting.

So much had happened since his last visit. How could things have been going so well and then suddenly stop? It didn't make sense. What did in his life anymore? He was buried in his sorrow and his past. He had nothing. It had all been taken from him in a few seconds–the length of time it took for a blood clot to dislodge from her leg and land in her lungs. And now...

He stepped forward and ran his hand across the top plank on the back. He reminded himself to be careful. They had taken home more than one splinter from the old bench. He tried to smile at the thought, but failed. He looked across the inlet toward Assateaque Island. He could see a small herd of wild horses roaming the beach, looking for their next bite of grass. He and Nancy used to sit and watch the horses for hours at a time. The ponies roamed the island day in and day out, nowhere to go, nothing to do but wait for that one time each summer when men on horses rounded them up and herded them across the channel to the mainland where they were auctioned off to raise money for the local fire department. The pony swim was an annual event for the community. It was a new beginning... a new life for the ponies.

Adam turned to face the back of Harrison's. As usual, the kitchen door was open. The aromas reminded him of how he and Nancy often pretended ordering their meal and having it served to them on their bench. They often debated what they were going to have. Fish? Seafood? Chicken? So many smells. So many choices. It was a silly game, but it was fun. He started to sit down, but stopped. It wouldn't be the same without her. Nothing was. He looked across the inlet again. His eyes teared. The horses were still there, waiting for their annual swim. He took in a deep breath. What was Nancy going to choose to have for dinner tonight? What was he?

Thoughts and tears stopped. He closed his eyes. The lyrics from the night before again returned. *The song I wish I sang...* Again, his hand rubbed across the top of the weathered wood. No splinters the first time, he repeated the action. Still no splinters. He leaned forward and spoke softly, "I love you, Nancy. I always will."

With that he did an about face and headed back towards the main Boardwalk. Turning northward, his pace quickened. There was a snap to his step. He stopped at Dumser's and had that milkshake. He took the top off and threw the straw away, drinking the thick liquid directly from the cup. He ignored the pink moustache just as he ignored a lot of things at that moment.

A jogger passed. You should stop and have an ice cream, Adam thought. To his surprise the man did. Ahead, he could see more low riders, another jogger and a couple of multi-people carts. In the distance, coming directly towards him, was a family all riding together... all on those old style Boardwalk rental bikes. The smile that he had been carrying since saying good-by to Nancy widened. He looked around. The shadows across the Boardwalk were deepening as the sun was now an hour off the western horizon. There was an increased chill in the air. The breeze had kicked up a notch. The smell... yes, the smell of the ocean was more intense. Stores were showing signs of closing. Yet in spite of the darkness that was slowly engulfing the area, Adam knew that OC was coming to life after a hard cold winter.

Other things were coming to life as well.

He took another big gulp of his shake and turned into a jewelry store. It was time for a new watch.

21

The next day

They had been walking at a brisk pace for the last mile. Mel knew it was a mile because she had been watching the signs posted on the light poles. The last time she was on the Boardwalk, the distance markers were painted right on the deck itself. That wasn't the only change, however. There were new benches, new lights and new store fronts mixed in amongst familiar names. She could tell where small sections of the Boardwalk had been replaced. She had been able to take all this in as Adam was his normal quiet self.

Unlike the night before, when he came into the bar with a burst of energy. He sat down next to her, ordered his V.O. and immediately starting talking. In the middle of this and before he got anything worthwhile out, he stopped. He stared at her a long moment, and then leaned forward and kissed her... right on the lips no less. While it was a short kiss, she sensed something about it... something special... something important. It definitely wasn't one of those *hey, how you doing* pecks she was so accustomed to by other patrons at the bar. When the kiss was over, he said, "are you busy tomorrow?"

"I'm booked in the morning," she said after collecting her thoughts. "The afternoon's slow."

"What time will you be finished?"

"My last appointment is at 2:00. It's for a cut only so I should be done around 2:30."

"Perfect. Will you go somewhere with me?"

She was again caught off guard. "Where?"

"The Boardwalk."

"The Boardwalk!" She started to ask why, but caught herself. If he wanted her to know, he would tell her.

Now, Adam still hadn't given a reason for the journey. She didn't mind. It was a beautiful spring afternoon. The breeze was light and the temperature had risen a few degrees from the day before. She looked across the beach. There were groups of people scattered around. Some were sunbathing. Others were sitting, talking or laying back to read. She smiled to herself. She knew people who wouldn't touch a book for months, and then come to the beach and read three books in three days.

Their journey south continued. They walked side by side. Adam occasionally put his hand on her arm to guide her away from an impending collision with missiles, as he came to call any peddled object. When they did talk, it was nothing of importance... the weather, local news, the upcoming season. She mentioned she hoped the area had a better season than the year before. He commented he suspected they would.

As they approached the more congested area, their pace slowed. At first she figured it was simply because the crowd was heavier, the missiles more frequent. But then she noticed a change in his demeanor. He became quieter, like he was nervous about something. He had stopped looking around and stared straight ahead. She suspected the *why* of the journey was soon to be answered. She inched closer to him and curled her arm through his. He responded by taking his other hand and laying it atop hers. His eyes, however, remained straight ahead.

They passed the Kite Loft and they passed Thrashers. They passed the old souvenir shop and Dumser's. As they started the incline up to the museum and the end of the Boardwalk, their pace slowed again. His grip on her hand tightened. They turned and went by the series of shops. Somewhat surprising, they didn't go into any. Instead, they walked to the end, turned and went around to the back of Harrison's. A couple more steps and Adam stopped. She looked at him. Tears had formed. His gaze turned downward. She followed his line of sight. He was looking at an old bench. It was obvious this was the destination of their journey. It was also obvious this bench meant something special to Adam.

She surmised it had something to do with his late wife, Nancy.

She felt a sense of sadness mixed with a sense of joy... joy that Adam was willing to share this with her. No one can ever claim they know how another person feels when they lose a loved one. She could at least claim being in the same ball-park. While the specifics of their tragedies were different, they were still tragedies.

Adam spoke in a soft voice. "This was our bench, Mel. This is where so many important things in our life took place. We first came here when we were in high school. I kissed her the first time here. It was late at night. The moon was brighter than I had ever seen. And we kissed."

He took in a deep breath and subconsciously wiped away a few tears. "Years later, this is where I asked her to marry me. It was a full moon that night, too." He again paused, obviously struggling to maintain control. "The funny thing is that every time we were here, Nancy managed to get a splinter in her backside. It was almost like a ritual... something to be expected... something to look forward to. Except the last time, she didn't get a splinter. We sat here and ate an ice cream. As we got up to leave, I inquired about the splinter. She told me no, she didn't get one this time. I commented that was sad. To which she turned to me and replied, 'no, Adam dearest, I didn't get a splinter in my butt today. But I do have something else growing in my belly.'" His voice started to tremble. "It was the last time we were here. It was the last time I was here... until yesterday."

He turned and faced her. There was a sense of renewed strength in his expression. "Mel, there's so much I want to say, there's so much I want to tell you. But if you're uncomfortable with this, I understand."

Mel wiped her own tears and kissed him lightly on the cheek. "I'd be honored to listen."

Adam's gaze returned to the bench. "When Nancy died, it was like the end of the world for me. The flight home from Africa was the longest of my life. When I finally arrived, I realized there wasn't anything I could do. The best hospital in the world couldn't bring Nancy back to me." He wiped a hand across his eyes. "As far as our baby, Nancy was only in her first trimester, so there wasn't much they could do there either. So not only did I lose Nancy, I lost our future. Again, it was like the end of the world. So what did I do? I ended my world as I knew it." His hand reached out and touched the back of the bench. "They say time heals all wounds. Time doesn't heal anything. The wounds never heal; you just learn to live with them... kind of like Bobby talking about bars.

Anyway, time passed, and I guess I did learn to live with the pain. I started going out, I started walking. I'd walk for hours at a time, sometimes just around my development. Sometimes I'd go up to Fenwick and walk the beach. The only thing that stopped me was the weather. I did get caught in a snow storm once... Pretty strange too, seeing it snow on the beach. One day I walked up Route 54. I spotted your place and went in. I remember the flowers on the table. Nancy loved fresh cut flowers." Adam paused. "That morning was the most contact I had with another human being in over a year. I guess I realized the world may have ended as I knew it, but another world was out there somewhere." Adam smiled slightly. "Its name was Smitty McGee's." The smile faded. "It was there I started to learn things I never knew before. It was a whole new language for me and Bobby was the teacher. In a very subtle way, he taught me the difference between loneliness and being alone. He taught me that life does end, but it can begin again. Everybody in the world has problems–bars as he calls them. It's how you handle these bars that makes the difference... And yes, we both give a damn about our kids." The smile returned. He looked up and pointed out across the inlet. "When I was here yesterday, I watched the horses as they grazed along the beach. Their lives are simple. They eat. I guess they sleep. And they wait to be herded up and moved across to Chincoteague where they begin a new life."

"I was talking with one of the regulars a few

nights ago–I don't even remember what we were talking about–but the conversation ended with the statement that there's always an alternative. The ponies may not have a choice whether to swim or not, but we do."

Adam took in a deep breath. "Standing here yesterday afternoon, looking at the bench and then looking out across the inlet, I realized Bobby was telling me one more thing–it was time I got on with my life. He gave me a shot of vodka one night instead of B&B. I thought he was just being funny until he told me I needed to learn how to acquire a taste for something different. Or as you said so eloquently one time, I had to learn how to dream again. Otherwise..." His gaze turned to Mel. "Otherwise I'd be singing the song we heard the other night: *the song I wish I sang, the story I wish I told.*"

They stood silently a few moments. "Would you like to sit down?" Adam offered.

"No, I don't think so. This is your and Nancy's bench," Mel said. "Maybe in time, we'll find a bench of our own."

"I'd like that," Adam said.

She stared into his eyes. "Would you really?"

Adam smiled through the tears. "Yes, I would."

She leaned in and kissed him lightly on the lips. "You know, Adam, if I may be so bold, I have an idea."

"Okay."

She looked down at the bench. "While I never had the pleasure of meeting Nancy, I bet she would like one of those *In Memory Of* plaques."

Adam stared at the bench himself. "Yes, I think she would. Thank you."

He wrapped his arm around her waist and led her away.

*****

He led her away–away from one world and into another. They took their time on this journey, stopping for a milkshake and a slice of pizza. Dessert was a shared box of popcorn. By the time they made it back to Adam's Jeep, the sun had finished its task for the day. The chill of the night air was just beginning. The beach was empty. Most of those still on the Boardwalk now wore sweaters or sweatshirts. She and Adam had neither, but that was okay. His arms were around her and hers around him. She hadn't felt this warm in a long time.

They drove up Coastal Highway in silence. Where they were going, she wasn't sure. But her womanly instincts were wide awake. He took her to his place. He led her into the house. He poured her a glass of wine, and then he kissed her. It was a kiss of passion.

Then he led her into the bedroom, where they

swam with the ponies.

*****

Bobby saw them come in and wiped off the area just vacated. Setting a glass of wine in front of Mel and a V.O. before Adam, he realized they came in together. That was a first! "Where have you two been?" he said, his eyebrows rising.

"Are you my mother?" Adam replied.

Bobby laughed at the uncharacteristic comment.

"We were on the Boardwalk," Mel said before anything else could be surmised.

"The Boardwalk?"

"Yeah, that's that long pier that runs along the beach in Ocean City," Adam said.

Bobby laughed again. "Something sure got in your gizzard tonight, didn't it?"

"You just mind yourself, Bobby, and attend to your customers over there." Mel pointed to where a trio of semi-regulars were just sitting down.

Appropriately distracted, Bobby did as he was told.

Adam held his glass up in a toast. "Cheers."

"Cheers," Mel repeated. She set her glass down and turned in her seat. The band was returning to their places after a break. Ricky caught her eye and held his hand up as if holding a mike. She started to nod in the negative, but stopped short. She looked over at Adam, who was watching Bobby serve the two new guests. She put her arm around his neck and pulled him to her. Kissing him on the cheek, she said, "You've given me so much tonight, maybe I can give you a little something in return. I'll be back."

Adam turned to see Mel standing next to Ricky. She looked at him, broadcasting a smile. As she started singing, it took Adam a moment to recognize the melody. It was the same song she had been humming the first day in the salon and had hummed several times since.

People, people who need people are the luckiest people in the world.

*****

Were there really people who needed people? Were there people who needed him? Two in particular came to mind... a set of twins. The thought continued to gnaw at him throughout the evening. He started to ask Mel about it on a couple occasions. The third time he finally found the courage. He leaned toward her and spoke softly. "Carol, my administrative assistant came to see me the other day. It was a surprise visit, but it was still good to see her. She came to see how I was doing. In addition..." He hesitated. "There's a set of conjoined twins out in UCLA."

Mel, who had been watching the band, turned to face him. "Tell me about them," she encouraged.

He did. When he finished, she took a sip of her wine and said, "are you asking me for advice?"

Adam nodded. She leaned forward and kissed him gently on the lips. "I think we just took another big step together, didn't we?"

He smiled meekly.

Another sip of wine, and she spoke. "Well, Dr. Adam Singer, I know brains are your specialty, but on this occasion I think you should go with what's in your heart." She leaned forward and kissed him again. "Let's go home and we can talk about it some more if you want."

And so they did.

22

Three days later

Adam slowed his pace as the crowd up ahead did the same in response to the security check point at the end of the corridor. It was the point at which the parking lot officially became the hospital. It was also the point where if you did not have a valid ID, you needed a pass. Rush hour at the John, they called it.

Adam had to give credit where credit was due, however. The line moved rather quickly compared to lines he waited in around the world. Terrorism was good for the security industry. When he finally made it to the head of the line, he saw that Eddie was on duty. Eddie was a tall thin black gentleman who had been there for eons–some claimed since the hospital was built. Besides towering over most people, he had piercing eyes. When he looked at you and asked the purpose of your visit, you dared not lie.

Focusing on the next person in line, Eddie started with the same verbiage. The words stopped as he recognized Adam. Eddie the security guard had never been a religious man–that is

Behind Bars

until Adam took a brain tumor out of his grand-
son's head. He was now a deacon at his church.
The burning stare quickly turned into a smile.
"Dr. Singer. Good morning, sir. So good to see
you. We've all missed you."

Adam tried not to blush, a common reaction
when such compliments were tossed his way.
"Thank you, Eddie. How's Anthony doing?"

That the famous doctor remembered his grand-
son's name made the security guard's smile even
wider. "Fine, sir. He'll graduate from high school
next year–that is if he keeps his mind on his
schoolwork and off the girls."

"Well, you tell Anthony I said he'd better graduate, because I don't want to be sitting in the
audience and him not go across that stage."

The smile now turned into an outright beam. "I
will tell him that, sir, I most certainly will." Eddie
knew that the doctor was true to his word. Rumor
had it, the doctor went to a lot of graduations.

Realizing he was now the cause for the delay in
the line, Adam said, "I'm just here for a meeting. I
suspect it won't take too long. I'll stop by on the
way out."

Eddie the security guard nodded and waved the
doctor through. "Again, sir, welcome back."

The *bowels of Hopkins*–the residents' term for
the first floor of winding, interlocking, confusing
as hell corridors–had not changed. The pictures
on the walls were the same–non-descript art, the

288

overhead florescent lights bright, and the floors shiny. But above all, there were people... people of all nationalities everywhere moving in different directions. To avoided recognition and thus having to stop for additional Eddie the security guard type conversations, Adam kept his head down. Except to avoid running into the person in front of him, he really didn't need to look where he was going anyway. His feet knew the way. He made it up to the conference room in the expected eleven and a half minutes–thirty seconds to spare.

*****

The Halsted conference room, while decorated on the inside with exquisite furniture and memorabilia representing the surgical history of the institution, was basically nondescript as one approached the polished oak doors. A small plaque on the wall was the only clue of what lie beyond. Adam glanced at his watch as he pushed open the left door. It was an instinctive habit developed over the years from expecting his residents to be on time. There was a small unfurnished outer office which served as a place for hanging one's coat; or if you were wearing a white coat, making sure it was properly buttoned. With no one in the outer office, Adam hurried through a second set of doors, afraid that if he didn't do it while he had the momentum, he would never go forward at all.

The conference room was everything he remembered. Like the bowels of Hopkins five stories below, nothing had changed. He turned his attention to the long mahogany table that sat in the middle. As he always did in reverence to those great surgeons who had sat at the table before him, he paused a moment and closed his eyes. When he opened them, he realized the twenty plus chairs were all full of men and women in white coats, all correctly buttoned of course. He also noticed that the room was relatively quiet. As he stepped forward, however, the noise level rose as chairs were pushed back and the men and women of the Johns Hopkins surgical conjoined twins team rose to their feet. People standing when he entered a room was one of the more unusual phenomena of fame, and one he never got used to. A smile crossed his face as a thought crossed his mind.

No one ever rose to their feet when he entered Smitty McGee's.

Verbal greetings were exchanged. Hands were shaken. There were pats on the back and even a few '*welcome backs*'. Old acquaintances were renewed. Not much else was said. After all, what do you say when so much time has passed, so much has changed in one's life? But Adam put on his game face–a wide smile and strong handshake. As he made his way around the room, he felt like the

President of the United States making his way towards the podium to give the State of the Union Address.

Then he realized in many ways, that's exactly what he was doing. He was making his way to the head of the conference table where all eyes would be focused on him, waiting to hear what he had to say, waiting to see the state of his mind, the state of his capacity to continue the work he had started a decade ago. While no one in the room needed the work, the surgical conjoined twins team was their passion. They were like a disaster response team waiting for the next set of twins Velcroed together in one form or another.

Adam made his way to where Dr. Fitzgerald was waiting for him at the head of the long table. He noticed immediately that there was a folder sitting at the head of the table. The folder was unopened. Fitzgerald was standing by his usual chair to the right. It didn't register with Adam at the time.

Fitzgerald held out his hand. "What a pleasant surprise, Adam. Good to see you." The assistant chief of pediatric neurosurgery turned and motioned to the group. "We were just going over a case out at UCLA–a set of twins, a year and a half old, who may be candidates for separation."

"Carol told me a little about the case," Adam said.

"Did you have a chance to look at the films?"

Fitzgerald inquired.

Adam's head cocked to the side. Another *failure to register* incident crossed his mind. Adam shrugged it off, saying, "yes, I did."

There was a collective intake of air around the room.

"Sit down, Adam," Fitzgerald said. "We'll go over the case with you."

Adam looked at the one vacant chair. It was the chair so many esteemed surgeons had sat in before him. It was the chair his own mentor sat in so many times, listening to Adam and his fellow residents present cases, answer questions and be grilled unmercifully by the then Chief of the department. It was also the chair he had occupied in the same capacity.

Adam looked at Fitzgerald. The young man had a strange look on his face; one Adam did not recall having seen before. It was an expression of maturity, confidence, yet there was something else...

A cough from down the table broke his train of thought. Adam looked out across the table. They were all still standing, still waiting. Adam nodded and said, "why don't we all sit down. After all, we're going to be on our feet a long time for this one." Adam quickly sat down, opened the folder in front of him and added, "okay, let's hear what you've got."

*****

When the meeting ended two hours later, the members of the team filed out of the room. Additional handshakes and greetings were exchanged. As was customary, Dr. Fitzgerald stayed behind to discuss any other departmental issues that may have arisen. When the room was empty and the door closed, the two men took their respective seats. Usually, it was a very relaxing atmosphere. Today, however, there was obvious tension in the air.

The two men sat in silence, Daniel Fitzgerald looking at his boss, Adam staring down at the folder opened before him. Finally, the world renowned pediatric neurosurgeon looked up. "You are one son-of-a bitch, you know that, Daniel?" he said.

Dr. Fitzgerald started to respond before realizing he didn't quite know what to say. Dr. Singer had never spoken to him that way before. While Dr. Singer could chew you a new asshole with the best of them, he always did it in a professional manner... and never with foul language. "Sir?"

Adam had yet to show much of a facial expression of any manner. "You tricked me into coming here today. You, Carol and everyone else."

"Tricked you?"

"You have wax in your ears, Doctor?"

In spite of his surprise at Adam Singer's verbiage and accusations, and in spite of Fitzgerald's desire to remain polite and professional, the assistant chief could not hold back the laughter.

"What the..." Adam said, catching himself.

Regaining control, Fitzgerald said, "You know, sir, we sat in this room the past year and talked about you, wondering how you were doing, wondering if you were going to be okay. And yes, wondering if we would ever be a team again. As we finished, someone would always shout out: *anybody have wax in their ears today*? There were a lot of things about you we missed, Adam, but funny enough, comments such as that were near the top."

Adam started to speak, but for the first time in his career, Fitzgerald held up a hand to silence his boss. His own facial expression turned serious. "One of the things we talked about was how to get you back. We were looking out for you; and yes, we were looking out for ourselves. But most of all, we were looking out for the work we do and the patients we do it on. When the case from UCLA came in and we first saw the original arteriogram, we knew..." Fitzgerald paused but did not break eye contact. "We knew we couldn't do it without you, Adam. There's no one else out there who could either. Every team in the country–the world for that matter–has turned the case down. Everybody says the cerebral blood vessels are too intertwined and there's too great a risk of not only losing one of the twins, but both. There's also concern the mass of vessels is expanding, which means if something's not done in the next few months... Adam, you're the only chance these kids have." Fitzgerald paused. "Because time was of the essence, the question of how to get you back became more pressing. On top of that, as I assume Carol has briefed you, the administration has started to make inquiries as to when you'd be back, or even if you'd be back. Anyway, we had a dilemma. Since you weren't here, and were actually the problem, finding a solution landed in my lap."

Adam started to speak; only Fitzgerald again hushed him with a hand motion. The assistant chief continued. "We both know that if I, or anyone else for that matter, simply came to you and asked for your help, you'd say no. So we had to find another way to get you here. I figured once that happened, we'd at least have a chance. So Carol and I came up with a plan."

Fitzgerald paused again, this time looking away for a moment. "You have said a lot of things to me over the years, sir, including inquiring about the wax in my ears on numerous occasions. There have been other moments as well. But the most memorable was the day you chastised me for something I did, or rather didn't do concerning a problem we were having with a couple of the residents. You recall what I'm talking about?"

Adam nodded yes.

Fitzgerald continued. "You told me that I was an excellent surgeon and knew medicine like no one you had ever met. Yet, you said that I couldn't critically think myself out of a wet paper bag. Well, that not only hurt, it dug deep into my soul, which I suspect was exactly your intention. So I took it to heart. After my ego recovered, I made a promise to myself. I said that one day I would prove to you I could indeed think myself out of a wet paper bag. You're here, so I guess I've accomplished that goal today."

Adam stared before a soft smile crossed his face. He nodded slightly. "When I saw you for the first time today, Fitz, I knew there was something different about you. When you held up your hand to hush me, I finally realized what it was. You finally grew a set of balls."

Fitzgerald tried not to laugh, but did. "You know Adam, the first person that comes up to me and says you haven't changed, I'm going to set them straight."

"You do that," Adam said. "Only they probably won't believe you."

Fitzgerald laughed again. Then his expression turned serious. "I have one question, if I may, sir?"

"My ears are clean."

Fitzgerald chuckled. "Tell me, how did you

know?"

"That this was a trick?"

Fitzgerald nodded.

"I didn't until I got here and you asked me if I saw the films. That sparked two clues. First, Carol came the beach to see me and acted like the visit was a secret. She basically implied that she thought you might need help and didn't realize it. Second, she brought me copies of the films and a summary of the case. When you asked me if I saw the films, that told me you knew I had them. I also realized Carol did not have the authority to take all that information out of the hospital without someone's permission, that someone being you. Another thing, when I came in here today, the chair at the head of the table was unoccupied and the folder was closed. It was a set up all the way, wasn't it?"

Fitzgerald looked hard at his boss. "I knew the only way I could get you back here was to make you think I was in trouble. Like I said earlier, if I simply came and asked…"

Adam stared back. Then a smile formed. "Like I said, Fitz, you've finally grown some balls."

Fitzgerald rose to his feet and extended his hand across the table.

Adam rose, took the outstretched hand, and said, "thank you, Fitz."

"You're welcome, sir."

"No, Daniel, I mean *thank you*."

Behind Bars

The assistant chief tipped his head to the side. Yes, the man was back. The team was again ready to play. "Welcome back, sir."

23

July 1, 2009

The sun had risen to allow light to squeeze through the space between the window drapes. The warmth settled on the face of the lone person spread eagled across the disheveled bed. He was at peace and in that state of sleep where dreams were frequent and vivid. Normally, he dreamed in black and white; this morning the visions were in color. His dream girl from months before had returned, causing him to emit a soft moan.

Somewhere in the distance he heard a banging noise. Someone was at the front door. His mind immediately reverted to a previous experience... a similar experience... he was with the same girl, too... wasn't he? He tried to refocus on what was going on around him, but it was difficult. The sounds outside his bedroom door continued. Soon he could hear feet–a lot of feet, and they were stampeding toward his door. Who let the animals out of their pen? And why did they always have to run so hard? Such little people, yet such loud feet.

Alerted by the activity, his dream girl began to

fade away. "Don't go," he begged. "You feel so good." Unfortunately, she didn't listen.

The noises grew louder. The herd was getting closer. He covered his eyes. His dream girl had disappeared completely.

There was a pounding on the bedroom door and the door burst open. The animals poured in. Without asking permission, all three piled onto the bed. "Uncle Bobby, Uncle Bobby," one of them shouted. There was so much noise... so much confusion. One of the animals started jumping up and down. "Ms. Mel's here. She's with some guy and some lady. She says we all need to get up and get packed. She says we're all going on a trip... a surprise trip."

He opened his eyes and sat up. He was surrounded by wild little animals, his little animals. Oh, how he loved them, bad timing and all. He looked toward the door.

Mel was standing there, a bright smile on her face. "Good morning, Coyote Ugly," she said.

Bobby wanted to flash her the bird, but caught himself in time. The animals were still around.

Mel stepped into the room and started waving her arms. "You kids go get packed," she directed. "We've got a plane to catch."

"A plane," one of the animals screamed. "We're going on a plane?"

Mel nodded yes. "But only if we get to the airport in time."

300

There was a scurry of activity as the three children rushed from the room.

Bobby was about to ask for an explanation, when he noticed Adam standing behind Mel. The doctor stepped forward. "Morning, Bobby."

"What the hell are you doing here?" Bobby asked. Then he noticed someone standing behind the good doctor. "Carol!" he said. Maybe his dream girl hadn't disappeared after all.

Carol stuck her head through the door. "Morning, Bobby."

"Would someone please tell me what's going on?" Bobby demanded.

"Get up and get dressed," Adam directed. "We have to be at the Salisbury airport in ninety minutes."

"Oh, yeah, and just where are we going?"

"California, my friend. California."

"And why California might I ask?"

"Several reasons," Mel injected. "Adam here is going to take me to one of those fancy hair salons like I always wanted. He says Jonathan is waiting for me."

"What!" Bobby exclaimed with disbelief.

Adam continued the explanation. "After that, we're all going to the beach to watch the sun set in the ocean."

"And then the next day," Mel added. "You, Carol and I are going to take the kids to Disneyland."

"No way," the bartender blurted. His head tilted

to the side as he looked directly at Adam. "Where you going to be?"

Adam stood silently a moment, a blank stare on his face. Mel grabbed his arm and said, "Dr. Singer here has a surgery to perform. Seems there's a set of twins waiting for him."

The infamous smile crossed Bobby's face. There was a long pause. Then, "you know, Doc, there's hope for you yet."

Adam ignored the comment, saying instead, "when we get back from our trip, you and me... you and I are going to write that book you always wanted."

"For real?"

"For real."

And so they...

And so we did.

THE END... or rather a new beginning.

OUTTAKES (*)

(*) The movies can do it. Why can't we?

From the *Go Figure* department:

Bobby pointed to a guy sitting at the other end of the bar. He leaned forward and spoke in a softer tone than usual. "See that guy down there? He just got out of prison this morning... federal prison no less. What does he do? He has his old lady bring him here for wings and an order of cheesy fries... go figure"

Motioning to a young man putting the moves on a young girl, Bobby said, "it's all about the timing, Adam. It's all about the timing."

Advice from your friendly bartender:

1) Don't take Nyquil and do shots.

2) Beware of cougars–older women on the prowl for unsuspecting young meat.

Mel leaned over to Adam and pointed at Bobby who was making his rounds up and down the bar. It was not only a busy night; it was a *thirsty* night, as people in the business called it when the average drink per person was high. The tip bucket was filling fast and Bobby's smile was widening with each donation to the cause. Mel said, "I've been to a lot of different places in my day and have seen a lot of different people working behind the bar. But there's no one with the swagger of Bobby."

Overheard at the bar: Sunny was a redneck with jewelry.

Bobby stopped and motioned to a foursome that had just bellied up to the bar. "What do you think about a golfer who carries a book of birds with him out on the golf course?"

"He probably likes birds," Adam replied.

"Or he can't play golf worth shit," Bobby countered. "Speaking of birds, how can you tell a woodpecker from other birds?"

"How?" Adam bit.

"They fuck up trees!"

Adam asked Bobby one evening, "Why do you put a lime in a bottle of Corona and an orange in a Blue Moon?"

Bobby replied instantly, "the lime in the Corona started in Mexico. It's put there to keep the spiders out of your beer."

"What about the orange in the Blue Moon?" Adam queried.

"Hell if I know." And then he was gone.

From the bartender's dictionary: *Dilligaf.* From Australia meaning: Do I look like I give a fuck? (Should be uttered just as part of a regular conversation.)

More advice from your friendly bartender:

1) Never brush your teeth before coming to the

bar. There isn't any drink anywhere that has toothpaste in it.

2) Never ask a bartender for a weak drink.

3) Never act like a bartender owes you a free drink.

4) The best thing you can tell a girl is no. They always want what they can't have.

Words of wisdom from Doug: You know if someone comes up behind you and sticks their finger in your ear by surprise, the sensation will stay with you for hours.

Overheard at the bar: two men sat drinking a beer and sharing a basket of wings. They were military police evidenced by their sweatshirts saying as much. It could also be ascertained if one listened closely that they were both sharpshooters. "What did you feel when you shot your first terrorist?" one man asked.

"A slight recoil," the other man answered.

A thought: Life is a terminal condition for which there is no cure.

Along similar lines, one of the regular older patrons came in one afternoon with a couple of his golfing buddies. He was popular in that he always had a pleasant disposition and was always good for a story or two. On this particular afternoon, he simply sat and sipped his drink–scotch and water, light on the water–and listened to his buddies lament about the disadvantages of growing old. Finally, after several minutes when it appeared the discussion was never going to end, he piped in with his two cents. He leaned into the bar, eyed his golf buddies and said, "you know, friends, it's better to be seen than to be viewed."

Overheard during the song, *Ride Sally Ride,* an older gentleman sitting a couple of stools down from Adam said, "Ride Sally ride. What's she riding?"

The gentleman next to Adam replied as he emptied his beer, "use your imagination, pal."

A piece of advice as to when you should stop drinking: If you are in the bathroom and cannot focus on *1.0 gpf 3.8 lpf,* you've probably had enough. (Ladies, you need to ask the guys about this one.)

From the *Go Figure* department:

Did you know that Jack Daniel's is one of the most recognized names in hard liquor and is made in Moore County, Tennessee? The plant is the oldest licensed distillery in the U.S. However, they can make it, but they can't sell it there. Moore County is dry, and has been since Prohibition. Go figure!

While on the topic of whisky, Bobby was pouring Adam a refill one evening, when the doctor said, "Hey, Bobby, what does V.O. stand for, anyway?"

Bobby looked at the bottle in hand and then at Adam, "fuck if I know."

Mel, who was waiting for the next trivia question to come up, leaned in their direction. "It stands for *very own*. Joseph Seagram created it for his son's wedding. It means very own blend."

The bartender and the doctor looked at one another, and then at the trivia queen. "She's smart," Adam said.

"You have no idea," Bobby added.

And finally (well, almost finally), do you know that one of the part-time bar backs at Smitty McGee's is a full-time IRS Agent? Go figure!

"I've always taught my residents that in surgery, you have to expect the unexpected," Adam said. "All the preparation in the world will not cover everything you're going to find once you're in the operating room."

"Expect the unexpected," Bobby repeated. "Guess you could say the same about life in general."

And finally (definitely finally), we'll let Doug the pontificator have the last word.

"Life is almost perfect," Doug bellowed out across the bar one night.

Most people laughed. Adam, however, remained stone-faced and watched Doug check out a couple (a cougar and her catch) sitting across the way. As the money was divided between the cash drawer and tip bucket, Adam said in a louder than normal voice, "what would make life perfect, Doug?"

The bartender paused and looked at Adam, the

inevitable grin replaced by a look of sadness. "If my dad was still here," he said.

And so the story ends (for now). Like we said in the beginning, it writes itself.

About the authors

 Jimmy is a Maryland native and an avid hunter and fisherman. He is a licensed charter boat captain and a licensed bartender.

 Dorsey, also a native of Maryland, is an avid fisherman and works as a medical consultant and clinically as a physician assistant.

This is their first book together. They are already working on the sequel, titled: *Secrets in the Sand.*

27249005R00187

Made in the USA
Lexington, KY
01 November 2013